"The blizzard will keep anybody from searching for us."

When she turned toward him, he didn't back away.

"I wanted you to know. I'm one of the good guys, and I'm not going to hurt you."

She'd heard that promise before. Other men had assured her that they wouldn't break her heart. The smart thing would be to step away, to put some distance between them. But they were awfully close. And he was awfully good-looking.

In spite of her resolution to steer clear of dangerous men, gently she reached up and rested her hand on his cheek. His stubble bristled under her fingers. Electricity crackled between them.

His hand clasped her waist as he lowered his head. His lips were firm. He used exactly the right amount of pressure for a perfect kiss.

She pulled away from him and opened her eyes. His smile was warm, his eyes inviting. *Perfect! Of course!* Guys like Cole—men who lived on the edge—made the best lovers.

"That was good," she said.

"I can do better."

CASSIE
MILES

MOUNTAIN
MIDWIFE

TORONTO • NEW YORK • LONDON
AMSTERDAM • PARIS • SYDNEY • HAMBURG
STOCKHOLM • ATHENS • TOKYO • MILAN • MADRID
PRAGUE • WARSAW • BUDAPEST • AUCKLAND

Here's to my buddy Cheryl.
And, as always, to Rick.

ISBN-13: 978-0-373-69522-5

MOUNTAIN MIDWIFE

This edition published by arrangement with Harlequin Books S.A.

For questions and comments about the quality of this book please contact us at Customer_eCare@Harlequin.ca.

www.eHarlequin.com

Printed in U.S.A.

ABOUT THE AUTHOR

Though born in Chicago and raised in L.A., Cassie Miles has lived in Colorado long enough to be considered a semi-native. The first home she owned was a log cabin in the mountains overlooking Elk Creek, with a thirty-mile commute to her work at the Denver Post.

After raising two daughters and cooking tons of macaroni and cheese for her family, Cassie is trying to be more adventurous in her culinary efforts. Ceviche, anyone? She's discovered that almost anything tastes better with wine. When she's not plotting Harlequin Intrigue books, Cassie likes to hang out at the Denver Botanical Gardens near her high-rise home.

Books by Cassie Miles

HARLEQUIN INTRIGUE

904—UNDERCOVER COLORADO*
910—MURDER ON THE MOUNTAIN**
948—FOOTPRINTS IN THE SNOW
978—PROTECTIVE CONFINEMENT†
984—COMPROMISED SECURITY†
999—NAVAJO ECHOES
1025—CHRISTMAS COVER-UP
1048—MYSTERIOUS MILLIONAIRE
1074—IN THE MANOR WITH THE MILLIONAIRE
1102—CHRISTMAS CRIME IN COLORADO
1126—CRIMINALLY HANDSOME
1165—COLORADO ABDUCTION*
1171—BODYGUARD UNDER THE MISTLETOE*
1177—SECLUDED WITH THE COWBOY*
1193—INDESTRUCTIBLE
1223—LOCK, STOCK AND SECRET BABY††
1229—HOOK, LINE AND SHOTGUN BRIDE††
1255—MOUNTAIN MIDWIFE

**Rocky Mountain Safe House
†Safe House: Mesa Verde
*Christmas at the Carlisles'
††Special Delivery Babies

CAST OF CHARACTERS

Rachel Devon—After a devastating career as an EMT and relationships gone wrong, the thirty-one-year-old nurse-midwife moves to the mountains looking for solitude and serenity.

Cole McClure—An undercover FBI agent from L.A., he hates the mountains. Betrayed by his superiors and pursued by a master criminal, he fights through a blizzard to protect a newborn.

Penny Richards—Nine months pregnant, she's given up every bad habit that would threaten her baby, except for robbing a casino.

Goldie Richards—In the first twenty-four hours of the baby's life, she's been shot at, pursued and threatened.

Ruby Richards—Penny's mother and Goldie's grandmother, she is more deeply involved in crime than she knows.

Jim Loughlin—The Grand County deputy sheriff will do anything to help the midwife who helped deliver his baby.

Frank Loeb—A sadistic thug, he won't let a bullet stop him from finding his share of the loot.

Wayne Prescott—The field agent in charge of the Colorado FBI office does his best to find his undercover agent.

Jenna Cambridge—Penny's best friend, she's a high school economics teacher in Granby with a good head for numbers.

Xavier Romero—A former snitch who owns the Stampede casino in Black Hawk.

Baron—The mysterious criminal mastermind uses gangs of underlings to rob banks and casinos.

Chapter One

Some babies are yanked into the world, kicking and screaming. Others gasp. Others fling open their little arms and grab. Every infant is unique. Every birth, a miracle.

Rachel Devon loved being a midwife.

She smiled down at the newborn swaddled in her arms. The baby girl—only two hours old—stared at the winter sunlight outside the cabin window. What would she be when she grew up? Where would she travel? Would she find love? *Good luck with that, sweet girl. I'm still looking.*

Returning to the brass bed where the mom lay in a state of euphoric exhaustion, Rachel announced, "She's seven pounds, six ounces."

"Totally healthy? Nothing to worry about?"

"A nine-point-five on the Apgar scale. You did good, Sarah."

"We did. You and me and Jim and..." Sarah frowned. "We still haven't decided on the baby's name."

Voices rose from the downstairs of the two-story log house near Shadow Mountain Lake. Moments ago, someone else had arrived, and Rachel hoped the visitor hadn't blocked her van in the circular driveway. After guiding Sarah through five hours of labor, aiding in the actual birth and taking another two hours with cleanup and postpartum instruction, Rachel was anxious to get home. "It's time for me to go. Should I invite whoever is downstairs to come up here?"

"Jim's mother." Sarah pushed her hair—still damp from the shower—off her forehead. "I'd like a bit more time alone. Would you mind introducing the baby to her grandma?"

"My pleasure. If you need anything over the next few days, call the Rocky Mountain Women's Clinic. I'll be on vacation, but somebody can help you. And if you really need to talk to me, I can be reached."

Sarah offered a tired smile. "I apologize in advance for anything Jim's mother might say."

"That sounds ominous."

"Let's just say there was a reason we didn't want Katherine here during labor."

Rachel descended the staircase and handed the baby girl to her grandmother, who had positioned herself in a rocking chair beside the moss rock fireplace. With her bright red hair and sleek figure, Katherine seemed too young to be a granny.

After a moment of nuzzling the baby, she shot Rachel a glare. "I wasn't in favor of this, you know. In my day, this wasn't the way we had babies."

Really? In your day, were babies delivered by stork?

Katherine continued, "Sarah should have been in a hospital. What if there had been complications?"

"Everything was perfect." Jim Loughlin reached down and fondly stroked his baby's rosy cheek. His hands were huge. A big, muscular guy, Jim was a deputy with the Grand County sheriff's department. "We wanted a home birth, and Rachel had everything under control."

Skeptically, Katherine looked her up and down. "I'm sorry, dear, but you're so young."

"Thirty-one," Rachel said.

"Oh my, I would have guessed eight years younger. The pixie hairdo is very flattering with your dark hair."

Her age and her hairstyle had nothing to do with her qualifications, and Rachel was too tired to be tactful. "If there had been complications, I would have been prepared. My training as a certified nurse-midwife is the equivalent of a master's degree in nursing. Plus, I was an EMT and ambulance driver. I'm a real good person to have around in any sort of medical emergency."

Katherine didn't give up. "Have you ever lost a patient?"

"Not as a midwife." A familiar ache tightened her gut. Rescuing accident victims was a whole other story—one she avoided thinking about.

"Leave Rachel alone," Jim said. "We have something else to worry about. The baby's name. Which do you like? Caitlyn, Chloe or Cameron?"

His mother sat up straight. "Katherine is a nice name. Maybe she'll have red hair like me."

Rachel eased her way toward the door. Her work here was done. "I'm going to grab my coat and head out."

Jim rushed over and enveloped her in a bear hug. "We love you, Rachel."

"Back at you."

This had been a satisfying home birth—one she would remember with pleasure. Midwifery was so much happier than emergency medicine. She remembered Katherine's question. *Have you ever lost a patient?* Though she knew that not everyone was meant to survive, her memories of victims she couldn't save haunted her.

As she stepped outside onto the porch, she turned up the fur-lined collar of her subzero parka. Vagrant snowflakes melted as they hit her cheeks. She'd already brushed the snow off the windshield and repacked her equipment in the back of the panel van with the Rocky Mountain Women's Clinic logo on the side. Ready to roll, Rachel got behind the steering wheel and turned on the windshield wipers.

Heavy snow clouds had begun to blot out the sun. The weatherman was predicting a blizzard starting tonight or tomorrow morning. She wanted to hurry home to her condo in Granby, about forty-five minutes away. Skirting around Katherine's SUV, she drove carefully down the steep driveway to a two-lane road that hadn't been plowed since early this morning. There were other tire tracks in the snow, but not many.

After a sharp left, she drove a couple hundred yards to a stop sign and feathered the brakes until she came to a complete stop.

From the back of the van, she heard a noise. Something loose rattling around? She turned to look. A man in a black leather jacket and a ski mask moved forward. He pressed the nose of his gun against her neck.

"Do as I say," he growled, "and you won't be hurt."

"What do you want?"

"You. We need a baby doctor."

A second man, also masked, lurked behind him in her van.

The cold muzzle of the gun pushed against her bare skin. The metallic stink of cordite rose to her nostrils. This weapon had been recently fired.

"Get out of your seat," he ordered. "I'm driving."

Fighting panic, she gripped the steering wheel. "It's my van. I'll drive. Just tell me where we're going."

From the back, she heard a grumble. "We don't have time for this."

The man with the gun reached forward and engaged the

emergency brake. "There's a woman in labor who needs you. Are you going to turn your back on her?"

"No," she said hesitantly.

"I don't want you to know where we're going. Understand? That's why you can't drive."

"All right. I'll sit in the back." Her van was stocked with a number of medical supplies that could be used as weapons—scalpels, scissors, a heavy oxygen tank. "I'll do what you say. I don't want any trouble."

"Get in the passenger seat."

Still thinking about escape, she unfastened her seat belt and changed seats. Her purse was on the floor. If she could get her hands on her cell phone, she could call for help.

The man with the gun climbed into the driver's seat. She noticed that his jeans were stained with blood.

His partner took his place between the seats. Roughly, he grabbed her hands and clicked on a set of handcuffs. Using a bandage from her own supplies, he blindfolded her.

The van lurched forward. Only a moment later, they stopped. The rear door opened and slammed shut. She assumed that the second man had left. Now might be her best chance to escape; she was still close enough to the cabin to run back there. Jim was a deputy and would know how to help her.

She twisted in the passenger seat. Before her fingers touched the door handle, the man in the driver's seat pulled her shoulders back and wrapped the seat belt across her chest, neatly and effectively securing her into place.

"Who are you?" she demanded.

He said nothing. The van was in motion again.

She warned, "You won't get away with this. There are people who will come after me."

He remained silent, and her tension grew. She'd been

lying about people looking for her. Tomorrow was the first day of a week vacation and she'd already called in with the information about Jim and Sarah's baby. Rachel lived alone; nobody would miss her for a while.

The blindfold made her claustrophobic, but if she looked down her nose, she could see her hands, cuffed in her lap. Helpless. Her only weapon was her voice.

She knew that it was important to humanize herself to her captor. If he saw her as a person, he'd be less likely to hurt her. At least, that was what the police advised for victims of kidnap. *Am I a victim?* Damn, she hoped not.

An adrenaline rush hyped her heart rate, but she kept her voice calm. "Please tell me your name."

"It's Cole," he said.

"Cole," she repeated. "And your friend?"

"Frank."

Monosyllables didn't exactly count as a conversation, but it was something. "Listen, Cole. These cuffs are hurting my wrists. I'd really appreciate if you could take them off. I promise I won't cause trouble."

"The cuffs stay. And the blindfold."

"Please, Cole. You said you didn't want to hurt me."

Though she couldn't see him, she felt him staring at her.

"There's only one thing you need to know," he said. "There's a pregnant woman who needs you. Without your help, she and her baby will die."

As soon as he spoke, she realized that escape wasn't an option. No matter how much she wanted to run, she couldn't refuse to help. The fight went out of her. Her eyes squeezed shut behind the blindfold. More than being afraid for her own safety, she feared for the unknown woman and her unborn child.

COLE MCCLURE CONCENTRATED on the taillights of Frank Loeb's car. The route to their hideout was unfamiliar to him and complicated by a couple of switchbacks; he didn't want to waste time getting lost.

The decision to track down the midwife had been his. It was obvious that Penny wasn't going to make it without a hell of a lot more medical expertise than he or any of the other three men could provide.

Cole glanced at the blindfolded woman in the passenger seat. Her posture erect, she sat as still as a statue. Her fortitude impressed him. When he held the gun on her, she hadn't burst into tears or pleaded. A sensible woman, he thought. Too bad he couldn't explain to her that he was one of the good guys.

She cleared her throat. "Has the mother been having contractions?"

"Yes."

"How far apart?"

"It's hard to tell. She was shot in the left thigh and has been in pain."

She couldn't see through the blindfold, but her head turned toward him. "Shot?"

"A flesh wound. The bullet went straight through, but she lost blood."

"She needs a hospital, access to a surgeon, transfusions. My God, her body is probably in shock."

Cole couldn't have agreed more. "She won't let us take her to a doctor."

"You could make her go. You said she was weak."

"If she turns herself in at the hospital, she won't be released. Penny doesn't want to raise her baby in jail. Can you understand that, Rachel?"

"How do you know my name?"

In spite of her self-possessed attitude, he heard a note of

alarm in her voice. He didn't want to reveal more information than necessary, but she deserved an explanation.

"When I realized that we needed a midwife, I called the women's clinic and pretended to want a consultation with a midwife. They gave me your name and told me that you were with a woman in labor."

"But they wouldn't tell you the patient's name," Rachel said. "That's a breach of confidentiality."

"Frank hacked their computer." The big thug had a sophisticated skill set that almost made up for his tendency toward sadism. "After that, finding the address was easy."

When they discovered that Rachel had been sent to the home of Sarah and Jim Loughlin, it seemed like luck was finally on Cole's side. The cabin was only ten miles away from their hideout.

Frank Loeb had wanted to charge inside with guns blazing, but Cole convinced him it was better to move with subtlety and caution. Every law enforcement man and woman in the state of Colorado was already on the lookout for them. They didn't need more attention.

"You're the casino robbers," she said.

"I wish you hadn't figured that out."

"I'd be an idiot not to," she said. "It's all over the news. How much did you get away with? A hundred thousand dollars?"

Not even half that amount. "If you're smart, you won't mention the casino again."

He regretted dragging her into this situation. If Rachel could identify them, she was a threat. There was no way the others would release her unharmed.

Chapter Two

Though the blindfold prevented Rachel from seeing where they were going, the drive had taken less than twenty minutes. She knew they were still in the vicinity of Shadow Mountain Lake, still in Grand County. If she could figure out her location, she might somehow get a message to Jim, and he could coordinate her rescue through the sheriff's department.

The van door opened, and Cole took her arm, guiding her as she stumbled up a wood staircase. Looking down under the edge of the blindfold, she saw it had been partially cleared of snow. The porch was several paces across; this had to be a large house or a lodge.

She heard the front door open and felt a gush of warmth from inside. A man ordered, "Get the hell in here. Fast."

"What's the problem?" Cole asked.

"It's Penny. She's got a gun."

Rachel stifled a hysterical urge to laugh. Penny had to be every man's worst nightmare: a woman in labor with a firearm.

Inside the house, Cole held her arm and marched her across the room. He tapped on a door. "Penny? I'm coming in. I brought a midwife to help you."

As Rachel stepped into the bedroom, she was struck by a miasma of floral perfume, antiseptic and sweat.

Cole wasted no time in removing the blindfold and the handcuffs.

From the bed, Penny stared at her with hollow eyes smeared with makeup. Her skinny arm trembled with the effort of holding a revolver that looked as big as a canon. A flimsy nightgown covered her swollen breasts and ripe belly, but her pale legs were bare. The dressing on her thigh wound was bloodstained.

"I don't want drugs," Penny rasped. "This baby is going to be born healthy. Hear me?"

Rachel nodded. "Can I come closer?"

"Why?" Her eyes narrowed suspiciously. "What are you going to do?"

"I'm going to help you have this baby."

"First things first," Cole said. "Give me the gun."

"No way." Penny's breathing became more rapid. Her lips pulled back as she gritted her teeth. Her eyes squeezed shut.

Even wearing the ski mask, Cole looked nervous. "What's wrong?"

"A contraction," Rachel said.

A sob choked through Penny's lips. Still clutching the gun, she threw her head back, fighting the pain with every muscle in her body. She stayed that way for several seconds. Instead of a scream, she exhaled a gasp. "Damn it. This is going to get worse, isn't it?"

"Here's the thing about natural childbirth," Rachel said as she moved closer to the bed. "It's important for you to be comfortable and relaxed. My name is Rachel, by the way. How far apart are the contractions?"

"I'm not sure. Eight or ten minutes."

"First baby?"

"Yes."

Experience told Rachel that Penny wasn't anywhere

near the final stages of labor. They probably had several more hours to look forward to. "Can I take a look at that wound on your leg?"

"Whatever."

Rachel sat on the bed beside her and gently pulled the bandage back. In her work as an EMT, she'd dealt with gunshot wounds before. She could tell that the bullet had entered the back of Penny's leg—probably as she was running away—and exited through the front. The torn flesh was clumsily sutured and caked with dried blood. "It doesn't appear to be infected. Can you walk on it?"

Defiantly, Penny said, "Damn right I can."

"I'd like you to walk into the bathroom and take a bath. Treat yourself to a nice, long soak."

"I don't need pampering." Her raccoon eyes were fierce. "I can take the pain."

Rachel looked away from the gun barrel that was only inches from her cheek. She didn't like Penny, didn't like that she was a criminal on the run and definitely didn't like her attitude. But this woman was her patient now, and Rachel's goal was a successful delivery.

"I'm sure you're tough as nails, Penny." Rachel stood and stepped away from the bed. "But this isn't about you. It's about your baby. You need to conserve your strength so you're ready to push when the time comes."

Cole approached the opposite side of the bed. "Listen to her, Penny."

"Fine. I'll take a bath."

Rachel went to the open door to the adjoining bathroom. As she started the water in the tub, she peered through a large casement window, searching for landmarks that would give her a clue to their location. All she saw was rocks and trees with snow-laden boughs.

Penny hobbled into the bathroom, using Cole's arm for

support. As he guided her through the doorway, he deftly took the revolver from her hand.

"Hey," she protested.

"If you need it, I'll give it back."

Hoping to distract her, Rachel pointed to the swirling water. "Do you need help getting undressed?"

Penny glared at both of them. "Get out."

Before she left, Rachel instructed, "Leave the door unlocked so we can respond if you need help."

With Penny disarmed and bathing, Rachel turned to Cole. "I need fresh bedding and something comfortable for her to wear. It'd be nice to have some soft music."

"None of these procedures are medical," he said.

She leaned toward him and lowered her voice so Penny couldn't hear from the bathroom. "If I'd come in here and wrenched her knees apart for a vaginal exam, she would've blown my head off."

He blinked. His eyes were the only part of his face visible. "I guess you know what you're doing."

"In the back of my van, there are three cases and an oxygen tank. Bring all the equipment in here." She stripped the sheets off the bed. "And you can start boiling water."

"Hot water? Like in the frontier movies?"

"It's for tea," she said. "Raspberry leaf tea."

Instead of leaving her alone in the bedroom, he opened the door and barked orders. She tried to see beyond him, to figure out how many others were in the house. Not that it mattered. Even if Rachel could escape, she wouldn't leave Penny until she knew mother and baby were safe.

She went to the bathroom and opened the door a crack. "Penny, are you all right?"

Grudgingly, she said, "The water feels good."

"Some women choose to give birth in the tub."

"Naked? Forget it." Her tone had shifted from maniacal

to something resembling cooperation. "Is there something else I should do? Some kind of exercise?"

Her change in attitude boded well. A woman in labor needed to be able to trust the people around her. Giving birth wasn't a battle; it was a process.

"Relax," Rachel said. "Take your time. Wash your hair."

In the bedroom, Cole thrust the fresh sheets toward her. "Here you go."

"Would you help me make the bed?"

He went to the opposite side and unfolded the fitted bottom sheet of soft lavender cotton. He'd taken off his jacket and was wearing an untucked flannel shirt over a long-sleeved white thermal undershirt and jeans with splotches of blood on the thigh.

She pulled the sheet toward her side of the bed. "We're probably going to be here for hours. You might as well take off that stupid mask."

He straightened to his full height—a couple of inches over six feet—and stared for a moment before he peeled off the black knit mask and ran his fingers through his shaggy, brown hair.

Some women would have considered him handsome with his high cheekbones, firm chin and deep-set eyes of cognac brown. His jaw was rough with stubble that looked almost fashionable, and his smile was dazzling. "You're staring, Rachel. Memorizing my face?"

"Don't need to," she shot back. "I'm sure there are plenty of pictures of you on 'Wanted' posters."

"I said it before, and I'll say it again. I'm not going to hurt you."

"Apart from kidnapping me?"

"I won't apologize for that. Penny needs you."

Rather than answering her challenge, he had appealed

to her better instincts. Cole was smooth, all right. Probably a con man as well as a robber. Unfortunately, she had a bad habit of falling for dangerous men. *Not this time.*

"Don't bother being charming," she said. "I'm going to need your help with Penny, but I don't like you, Cole. I don't trust a single word that comes out of your mouth."

He grinned. "You think I'm charming."

Jerk! As she smoothed the sheets, she asked, "Which one of the men out there is the father of Penny's baby?"

"None of us."

Of course not. That would be too easy. "Can he be reached?"

"We're not on vacation here. This is a hideout. We don't need to invite visitors."

But this was a nice house—not a shack in the woods. Finding this supposed "hideout" that happened to be conveniently vacant was too much of a coincidence. "You must have planned to come here."

"Hell, no. We were supposed to be in Salt Lake City by now. When Penny went into labor, we had to stop. The house belongs to someone she knows."

The fact that Penny had contacts in this area might come in handy. Rachel needed to keep her ears and eyes open, to gather every bit of information that she could. There was no telling what might be useful.

By the time Penny got out of the tub, Rachel had transformed the bedroom into a clean, inviting space using supplies from her van. The bedding was fresh. A healing fragrance of eucalyptus and pine wafted from an herbal scent diffuser. Native American flute music rose from a CD player.

Before Penny got into bed, Rachel replaced the dressings on her leg wound, using an antiseptic salve to ease the pain. In her work as a nurse-midwife, she leavened various herbal and homeopathic methods with standard medical procedure. Basically, she did whatever worked.

Though Penny remained diffident, she looked young and vulnerable with the makeup washed off her face. Mostly, she seemed tired. The stress of labor and the trauma of being shot had taken their toll.

Rachel took her blood pressure, and she wasn't surprised that it was low. Penny's pulse was jumpy and weak.

When her next contraction hit, Rachel talked her through it. "You don't have to tough it out. If you need the release of yelling—"

"No," she snapped. "I'm not giving those bastards the satisfaction of hearing me scream."

Apparently, she was making up for her weakened physical condition with a powerful hostility. Rachel asked, "Should I send Cole out of the room while I do the vaginal exam?"

"Yes."

He was quick to leave. "I'll fetch the tea."

Alone with Penny, Rachel checked the cervix. Dilation was already at seven centimeters. This baby could be coming sooner than she'd thought. "You're doing a good job," she encouraged. "It won't be too much longer."

"Is my baby okay?"

"Let's check it out."

Usually, there was an implied trust between midwife and mom, but this situation was anything but usual. As Rachel hooked up the fetal monitor, she tried to be conversational. "When is your due date?"

"Two days from now."

"That's good. You carried to full term." At least, there shouldn't be the problems associated with premature birth. "Is there anything I ought to know about? Any special problems during your pregnancy?"

"I got fat."

Rachel did a double take before she realized Penny was joking. "Are you from around here?"

"We lived in Grand Lake for a while. I went to high school in Granby."

"That's where I live," Rachel said. "Is your family still in Grand Lake?"

"It's just me and my mom. My dad left when I was little. I never missed having him around." She touched her necklace and rubbed her thumb over the shiny black pearl. "Mom gave me this. It's her namesake—Pearl. She lives in Denver, but she's house-sitting for a friend in Grand Lake."

They weren't too far from there. Grand Lake was a small village—not much more than a main street of shops and lodging for tourists visiting the scenic lakeside. "Should I try to contact your mother?"

"Oh. My. God." Penny rolled her eyes. "If my mom knew what I was up to, she'd kill me."

Her jaw clenched, and Rachel talked her through the contraction. Penny must have had some Lamaze training because she knew the breathing techniques for dealing with the pain.

When she settled back against the pillows, she said, "If anything happens to me, I want my mom to have my baby."

"Not the father?"

"Mom's better." She chewed her lower lip. "She'll be a good grandma if I'm not around."

Considering a premature death wasn't the best way to go into labor. Rachel preferred to keep the mood upbeat and positive. "You're doing fine. Nothing bad is going to happen."

"Do you believe in premonitions? Like stuff with tarot cards and crystal balls?"

"Not really."

"My friend Jenna did a reading for me. Hey, maybe you know her. She lives in Granby, too. Jenna Cambridge?"

"The name isn't familiar."

"She's kind of quiet. Doesn't go out much," Penny said. "Every time I visit her, I try to fix her up. But she's stuck on some guy who dumped her a long time ago. What a waste! Everybody falls. The trick is to get back on the bicycle."

Though Rachel wasn't prone to taking advice from a pregnant criminal who didn't trust the father of her baby, she had to admit that Penny made a good point. "Doesn't do any good to sit around feeling down on yourself."

"Exactly." She threw up her hands. "Anyway, Jenna read my cards and told me that something bad was going to happen. My old life would be torn asunder. Those were her words. And she drew the death card."

Her friend Jenna sounded like a real peach. Pregnant women were stressed enough without dire warnings. "The death card could mean a change in your life. Like becoming a mom."

"Maybe you're right. I have changed. I took real good care of myself all through the pregnancy. No booze. No cigs. I did everything right."

Except robbing a casino. Rachel finished hooking up the monitor and read the electronic blips. "Your baby's heartbeat is strong and steady."

When Cole returned with the raspberry tea, Rachel moved into the familiar pattern of labor—a combination of her own expertise and the mother's natural instincts. Needing to move, Penny got out of the bed a couple of times and paced. When she complained of back pain, Cole volunteered to massage. His strong hands provided Penny with relief. He was turning out to be an excellent helper—uncomplaining and quick to follow her instructions.

When the urge to push came, Penny screamed for the first time. And she let go with a string of curses. Though Rachel had pretty much heard it all, she was surprised by the depth and variety of profanity from such a tiny woman.

Cole looked panicked. "Is this normal?"

"The pushing? Or the I-hate-men tirade?"

"Both."

"Very typical. I bet you're glad you took the gun away."

"Hell, yes."

A mere two hours after Rachel had arrived at the house, Penny gave birth to an average-sized baby girl with a healthy set of lungs.

Though Rachel had participated in well over two hundred births, this moment never failed to amaze her. The emergence of new life gave meaning to all existence.

Postpartum was also a time that required special attention on the part of the midwife. Penny was leaking blood onto the rubber sheet they'd spread across the bed. Hemorrhage was always a danger.

Rachel held the newborn toward Cole. "Take the baby. I need to deal with Penny."

Dumbstruck, he held the wriggling infant close to his chest. His gaze met hers. In his eyes, she saw a reflection of her own wonderment, and she appreciated his honest reverence for the miracle of life. For a tough guy, he was sensitive.

Her focus right now was on the mother. Rachel urged, "You need to push again."

"No way." With a sob, Penny covered her eyes with her forearm. "I can't."

She had to expel the afterbirth. As Rachel massaged the uterus, she felt the muscles contract, naturally doing what was necessary. The placenta slipped out. Gradually, the bleeding slowed and stopped.

Cole stood behind her shoulder, watching with concern. "Is she going to be okay?"

"They both are."

Penny forced herself into a sitting position with pillows behind her back. "I want my baby."

With Cole's help, Rachel clipped the cord, washed the infant and cleared her nose of mucus. The rest of the cleanup could wait. She settled the new baby on Penny's breast.

As mother and child cooed to each other, she turned toward Cole in time to see him swipe away a tear. Turning away, he said, "I'll tell the others."

"Whoa, there. You're not leaving me with all the mess to clean up."

"I'll be right back."

Rachel sank into a chair beside the bed and watched the bonding of mother and child. Though Penny hadn't seemed the least bit maternal, her expression was serene and gentle.

"Do you have a name?" Rachel asked.

"Goldie. She's my golden child."

From the other room, she heard the men arguing loudly. Catching bits of their conversation, Rachel got the idea that they were tired of waiting around. *Bad news for her.*

When the gang was on the run again, they had no further need for a midwife. She was afraid to think of what might happen next.

Chapter Three

In the bedroom, Cole stood at the window and looked out into a deep, dark forest. Fresh snow piled up on the sill. He could hardly believe that he was considering an escape into that freezing darkness. He lived in L.A., where his only contact with snow was the occasional snowboarding trip to Big Bear Lake. He hated the cold.

A month ago, when the FBI office in Denver tapped him for this undercover assignment, he'd tried to wriggle out of it. But they'd needed an agent who was an unfamiliar face in the western states. The operating theory was that someone inside the FBI was connected to the spree of casino and bank robberies.

He stepped away from the window and began repacking Rachel's medical equipment in the cases from her van. Both of the women were in the bathroom, chatting about benefits of breast feeding and how to use the pump. As he eavesdropped, he marveled at how normal their conversation sounded. For the moment, Penny wasn't a hardened criminal and Rachel wasn't a kidnap victim. They were just two women, talking about babies.

And he was just an average guy—shocked and amazed by the mysteries of childbirth. He didn't have words to describe how he'd felt when Goldie was born. He forgot where he was and why he was there. Watching the newborn take her first breath had amazed him. Her cry was the voice of an angel. Pure and innocent.

In that moment, he wanted to protect Penny instead of taking her into FBI custody.

And then there was Rachel. Slender but muscular, she moved with a natural grace. Her short, dark hair made her blue eyes look huge, even though she wasn't wearing any makeup. He felt guilty as hell for dragging her into this mess. Top priority for him was to make sure Rachel escaped unharmed.

From the bathroom, he overheard her say, "Your body needs time to recover, Penny. You should spend time in bed, relaxing."

"Don't worry. I'm not going anywhere."

"Will the men agree to let you sleep tonight?"

"They'll do what I say," Penny said airily. "They can't leave me behind."

"Why not?" Rachel asked.

"Because I'm the only one who knows where the money is hidden."

Cole feared that her confidence might be misplaced. Frank and the other two were anxious to get going. No doubt, they could force Penny to tell them about the stash from five different robberies in three states.

Rachel seemed to be thinking along the same lines. "What if they threaten you?"

"They wouldn't dare. My baby's father is the head honcho. The big boss. If anybody hurts me, they'll answer to him."

Cole held his breath. *Say his name, Penny.* He needed to know the identity of the criminal mastermind who controlled this gang and at least five others. They referred to him as Baron, and he was famous for taking bloody revenge on those who betrayed him. Cole's reason for joining this gang of misfits was to infiltrate the upper levels of the organization and get evidence that could be used against Baron.

Rachel asked, "Does he know about Goldie?"

"Don't you remember? I told you all about Baron, about how we met. Damn, Rachel. You should learn to pay attention."

"Sorry," she murmured.

"He loves me. After this job, he promised to take me home with him, to raise our baby."

"Is that what you want?"

"You bet it is." Penny giggled. "Want to know a secret? A little while ago, I called Baron and told him about Goldie. He's coming here. He ought to be here any minute."

Not good news. Cole might have been able to convince the others in the gang to release Rachel. These guys weren't killers, except for Frank. Baron was a different story; he wouldn't leave a witness alive.

From the bathroom, he heard Rachel ask, "How does he know where you are? Cole said this house wasn't a scheduled stop."

"Simple," Penny replied. "This is Baron's house."

That was all Cole needed to hear. He could find Baron's identity by checking property records. As far as he was concerned, his undercover assignment was over. He reached into his jeans pocket, took out his cell phone.

This wasn't an everyday cell. Though Cole didn't need a lot of fancy apps, he'd used the geniuses at the FBI to modify his phone to suit his specific needs.

The first modification: He could disable the GPS locator. Unless he had it turned on, he couldn't be tracked. His handler—Agent Ted Waxman in L.A.—wasn't thrilled with the need for secrecy, but Cole needed to be sure his cover wouldn't be blown by some federal agent jumping the gun.

Second, his directory of phone numbers couldn't be read without using a five-digit code. His identity was protected in case somebody picked up his phone.

Third and most important, his number was blocked to everyone. Waxman couldn't call him with new orders and information. Cole, alone, made the decision when he would make contact and when he needed help.

Now was that time. He activated the GPS locator to alert Waxman that he was ready for extraction. Response time was usually less than an hour. Cole intended to be away from the house when that time came.

He slid the phone into his pocket and called out, "Hey, ladies, I need some help figuring out how to pack this stuff."

Rachel came out of the bathroom. Right away, he could see the change in her demeanor. No longer the self-assured professional, she had a haunted look in her eyes. Beneath her wispy bangs, her forehead pinched with worry. She whispered, "What's going to happen to me?"

Now would have been a good time to flash a badge and tell her that he was FBI, but he wasn't carrying identification. "I'll get you out of here."

Her gaze assessed him. During the hours of Penny's labor and the aftermath, a bond had grown between them. He hoped it was enough to make her cooperate without the reassurance of his credentials.

She asked, "Why should I trust you?"

"You don't have much choice."

Penny swept into the room and went to the travel bassinette where her baby was sleeping. "Be sure that you put all the baby stuff in the huge backpack so I can take it with me."

"Like what?" Cole asked.

"Diapers," Rachel said. "There's a sling for carrying newborns. And you'll need blankets and formula."

"But I'm breast-feeding. My milk already came in. Does that mean my boobs are going to get small again? Jenna said they would."

"Your friend Jenna doesn't have children. She doesn't know." Rachel's hands trembled as she sorted through the various baby items. "I don't have a car seat I can leave with you. You'll need to buy one as soon as possible."

Cole saw an opportunity to get Rachel alone. He wanted to reassure her that help was on the way. He asked her, "Don't you have a baby seat in your van?"

"I want it." Penny climbed onto the bed and stretched out. Her pink flannel robe contrasted her wan complexion. "Get it for me."

Rachel said, "I need that car seat for emergencies. If I have to transport a child to a hospital or—"

"Don't be stupid, Rachel. You're not going to need that van anymore. You're coming with me. I need you to help me with Goldie."

Rachel recoiled as though she'd been slapped. "I have a job."

"So what? You'll make more money with me than you would as a midwife." Penny propped herself up on one elbow. "Come here and help me get these pillows arranged."

Rachel did as she'd been ordered, then she turned toward Cole. "I'll help you get the car seat out of the van. The straps are complicated, and I don't want you to break it."

From the bed, Penny waved. "Hurry back. I want more tea."

He grabbed Rachel's down parka from the bedroom

closet and held it for her. She hadn't said a word, but he knew she'd made a decision to stick with him. Not surprising. Trusting Penny to take care of her would be suicidal.

RACHEL DIDN'T HAVE A PLAN. Trust Cole? Sure, he'd shown sensitivity when the baby was delivered. The whole time he was helping her, he'd been smart and kind, even gentlemanly. But he also had kidnapped her and jammed a gun into her neck.

All she needed from him was her car keys.

When they stepped outside through the side door of the house, he caught hold of her arm and pulled her back, behind the bare branches of a bush and a towering pine. Edging uphill, he whispered, "Duck down and stay quiet. Something isn't right."

The night was still and cold. Snowflakes drifted lazily, and she was glad for the warmth of her parka and hood. Behind them was a steep, thickly forested hillside. Peeking around Cole's shoulder, she saw the side of the house and the edge of the wooden porch that stretched across the front. Since she'd been sequestered in the bedroom with Penny and hadn't seen the rest of the house, she hadn't realized that it was two stories with a slanted roof. To her right was a long, low garage. Was her van parked inside? She couldn't see past the house, didn't know if there was a road in front or other cars.

Through the stillness, she heard the rumble of voices. There were others out here, hiding in the darkness.

She whispered, "Can you see anything?"

"A couple of shadows. No headlights."

Mysterious figures creeping toward the hideout might actually be to her advantage. She prayed that it was the police who had finally tracked down the gang. "Who is it?"

"Can't tell." His voice was as quiet as the falling snow; she had to lean close to hear him. "Could be the cops. Or it could be Penny's boyfriend."

"Baron." He sounded like a real creep—much older than Penny and greedy enough to want his pregnant girlfriend to participate in a robbery. "Penny said this was his house. Why wouldn't he just walk inside?"

"Hush."

For a moment, she considered raising her hands above her head and marching to the front of the cabin to surrender. It was a risk, but anything would be better than being under Penny's thumb.

Gunfire from a semiautomatic weapon shattered the night. She heard breaking glass and shouts from inside the house.

She wasn't a stranger to violence. When she was driving the ambulance, she'd been thrust into a lot of dicey situations, and she prided herself on an ability to stay calm. But the gunfire shocked her.

Shots were returned from inside the house.

There was another burst from the attackers.

She clung to Cole's arm. "Tell me what to do."

"We wait."

The side door they'd come through flung open. Frank charged outside. With guns in both hands, the big man dashed into the open, firing wildly as he ran toward the garage.

He was shot. His arms flew into the air before he fell. His blood splattered in the snow. He didn't attempt to get up, but she saw his arm move. "He's not dead."

"Don't even think about stepping into the open to help him," Cole whispered. "The way I figure, there are only two shooters. Three at the most. They don't have the manpower to surround the cabin, but they have superior weapons."

Though her mind was barely able to comprehend what she was experiencing, she nodded.

He continued, "We'll go up the hill, wait until the shooting is over and circle back around to the garage."

Taking her gloved hand, he pulled her through the ankle-deep snow into the surrounding forest. Behind them, gunfire exploded. Anybody living within a mile of this house had to be aware that something terrible was happening. The police would have to respond.

Crouched behind a snow-covered boulder, Cole paused and looked back. "We're leaving tracks. They won't have any trouble following us. We need to go faster."

Her survival instinct was strong. She wanted to make a getaway, but there was something else at stake. "We can't leave Penny here. Or the baby."

A sliver of moonlight through clouds illuminated his face. In his eyes, she saw a struggle between protecting the innocent and saving his own butt. "Damn it, Rachel. You're right."

Sadly, she said, "I know."

They retraced their steps to the house. Instead of using the door, Cole went to the rear of the house. He stopped outside a window. Inside, she saw the bathroom where she and Penny had been talking only a little while ago.

He dug into his pocket, took out her car keys and handed them to her. "If anything happens to me, get the hell out of here. Hide in the forest until you can get back to the garage."

The car keys literally opened the door to her escape. Her purse was in the van. And her cell phone.

When he shoved the casement window open, she said, "All those windows were latched."

"I opened it hours ago," he said. "I expected to be escaping from the inside out. Not breaking in."

Walking into a shoot-out was insanity. But the alternative was worse. She couldn't leave a helpless newborn to the mercy of these violent men.

Cole slipped through the window, and she got in position to follow.

"No," he said. "Stay here."

There wasn't time to argue. He needed her help in handling Penny and the baby. She hoisted herself up and over the sill.

As soon as she was inside, she heard the baby crying. In the bedroom, Cole knelt beside Penny's body on the floor. She'd been shot in the chest. Her open eyes stared sightlessly at the ceiling.

Rachel reached past Cole to feel Penny's throat for a pulse. Her skin was still warm, but her heart had stopped. There was nothing. Not even a flutter. Penny was gone. After her heroic struggle to bring her baby into the world, she wouldn't live to see her child grow. Fate was cruel. Unfair. *Oh, God, this is so wrong.*

From the front of the house, the gun battle continued, but all she heard was the baby's cries. If it was the last thing she ever did, Rachel would rescue Goldie. Moving with purpose, she took the baby sling from the backpack. When she snuggled Goldie into the carrier, the infant's cries modified to a low whimpering.

Cole grabbed the backpack filled with baby supplies. They went through the bathroom window into the forest.

They were only a few steps into the trees when he signaled for her to stop. He said, "Do you hear that?"

She listened. "It's quiet."

The shooting had ended. The battle was over. Now the attackers would be coming after them.

Chapter Four

Cole went first, leading Rachel up the forested hill and away from the house. The cumbersome backpack hampered his usual gait. He hunched forward, moving as quickly as possible in the snow-covered terrain. Even if there had been a path through these trees, he wouldn't have been able to see it. Not in this darkness. Not with the snow falling.

His leather jacket wasn't the best thing to be wearing in this weather, but he wasn't cold. The opposite, in fact. He was sweating like a pig. Though breathing hard, he couldn't seem to get enough wind in his lungs. After only going a couple of hundred yards, his shoulders ached. His thigh muscles were burning. This high elevation was killing him. He estimated that they were more than eight thousand feet above sea level. What the hell was a California guy like him doing here? His natural habitat was palm trees.

He picked his way through the rugged trunks of pine trees and dodged around boulders. After he climbed over a fallen log, he turned to help Rachel. She had the baby in the sling, tucked inside her parka.

She ignored his outstretched hand and jumped over the log, nimble as a white-tailed deer.

"Careful," he said.

"I'm good."

Her energy annoyed him. Logically, he knew that Rachel lived here full-time and was acclimated to the altitude. But he wanted to be the strong one—the protector who would lead her and the baby to safety.

Hoping to buy a little time to catch his breath, he asked, "How's Goldie?"

Rachel peeked inside her parka. "Sleeping. She's snuggled against my chest and can hear my heartbeat. It probably feels like she's still in the womb."

They needed to find shelter soon. It couldn't be good for a newborn to be exposed to the cold.

"I have a question," she said. "Why are we going uphill?"

"Escape."

"If we go down to the road, we'll be more likely to find a cabin. Or we could flag down a passing car."

He looked down the hill. The lights from the house were barely visible. "We're going this way because we can't risk having the guys who attacked the house find us. They'll be watching the road."

"They'll be looking for us? Why?"

If the gunmen worked for Baron, they wouldn't leave without the boss man's baby. If they were Baron's enemies, the same rationale applied. Goldie was a valuable commodity. "It's not us they're after."

Her arm curled protectively around the infant. "The police ought to be here soon. Somebody must have reported all that gunfire."

It was too soon to expect a response from his GPS signal, but he trusted that the FBI was closing in on this location. "Nothing would please me more than hearing cop sirens."

"You can't mean that." Her earnest gaze confronted him. "You'll be taken into custody."

He'd almost forgotten that she still didn't know his identity. As far as Rachel was concerned, he was the guy who kidnapped her at gunpoint. An armed robber.

"If I got arrested, would you be heartbroken?"

She exhaled a puff of icy vapor. "No."

"Maybe a little sad?"

"Let me put it this way. I wouldn't turn you in."

Her response surprised him. He had her pegged as a strictly law-abiding citizen who'd be delighted to see any criminal behind bars. But she was willing to make an exception for him. Either she liked him or she had a dark side that she kept hidden.

He turned to face the uphill terrain. "We'll keep moving until we know we're safe. Then we can double back to the road."

The brief rest had allowed him to recover his strength. He slogged onward, wanting to put distance between them and the men with guns. In spite of the burn, his legs took on a steady rhythm as he climbed. Coming through a stand of trees, he realized that they'd reached the highest point on the hill. He maneuvered until he was standing on a boulder and waited for Rachel to join him.

"This is a good lookout point. Do you see anything?"

Together, they peered through the curtain of trees. The snowfall was thick. Heavy clouds had blocked out the light from the moon and stars.

"There." She pointed down the hill.

The beams of a couple of flashlights flickered in the darkness. They weren't far away. Maybe eighty yards. He and Rachel were within range of their semiautomatic weapons.

He ducked. She did the same.

The searchers were too close. His hope for escape vanished in the howling wind that sliced through the tree trunks. He and Rachel had left tracks in the snow that a blind man could follow. Peering over the edge of the boulder, he saw the flashlights moving closer. There was only one way out of this.

He slipped his arms out of the backpack. "Take the baby and run. Get as far away from here as you can."

"What are you going to do?"

"I'll distract them."

Going up against men with superior firepower wasn't as dumb as it sounded. Cole had the advantage of higher ground. If he waited until they got close, he might be able to take out one of them before the other responded.

"There's something you haven't considered," she said.

"What's that?"

"Snow."

While they'd been climbing, the full force of the impending blizzard had gathered. The storm had taken on a fierce intensity.

She grabbed his arm and tugged. "They won't be able to see us in the blizzard. The wind will cover our tracks."

Great. He wouldn't die in a hail of bullets. He'd freeze to death in a blizzard.

"Come on," she urged. "I need you. Goldie needs you."

He shouldered the pack again. Going downhill should have been easier, but his knees jolted with every step. At the foot of the slope, they approached an open area where the true velocity of the storm was apparent. The snow fell in sheets. His visibility was cut to only a few yards, but he figured they could cover more distance if they went straight ahead instead of weaving through the trees.

When he stepped into the open, he sank up to his knees. His jeans were wet. His fingers and toes were numb.

"Stay close to the trees," Rachel said. "It's not as deep."

At the edge of the forest, the snow was over his ankles. He trudged through it, making a path for her to follow. One minute turned into ten. Ten into twenty. Inside his boots, his feet felt like frozen blocks of ice. The snow stung his cheeks. So cold, so damned cold. If he was this miserable what was happening to Goldie? Fear for the motherless newborn kept him moving forward. He had to protect this child, had to find shelter.

But he'd lost all sense of direction in the snow. As far as he could tell, they might be heading back toward the house.

Trying to get his bearings, he looked over his shoulder. He doubted that the bad guys were still in pursuit. Any sane person would have turned back by now.

As Rachel had predicted, the snows were already drifting, neatly erasing their tracks.

He couldn't tell how far they'd gone. It felt like miles, endless miles. Needing a break, he stepped back into the shelter of the forest. His chest ached with the effort of breathing. His eyes were stinging. He squeezed his eyelids shut and opened them again. Squinting, he looked through the trees and saw a solid shape. A cabin. He blinked, hoping that his brain wasn't playing tricks on him. "Rachel, do you see it?"

"A cabin." Her voice trembled on the edge of a sob. "Thank God, it's a cabin."

He helped her up the small embankment, and they approached the rear of the cabin. No lights shone from inside.

The front door was sheltered by a small porch. Cole

hammered against the green painted door with his frozen fist. No answer. Nobody home.

He tried the door handle and found it locked. He was carrying lock picks, but it was too cold to try a delicate manipulation of lock tumblers. He stepped back, prepared to use his body as a battering ram.

"Wait," Rachel said. "Run your hand over the top sill. They might have left a key."

"We need to get inside." He was too damned cold and tired to perform a subtle search. "Why the hell would anybody bother to lock up and then leave a key?"

"This isn't the city," she said. "Some of these little cabins are weekend getaways with different families coming and going. Give it a try."

He peeled off his glove. His fingers were wet and stiff, but he didn't see the whitened skin indicating the first stage of frostbite. When he felt along the ledge above the door, he touched a key. It seemed that their luck had turned.

Shivering, he fitted the key into the lock and pushed open the door. He and Rachel tumbled inside. When he shut the door against the elements, an ominous silence wrapped around them.

RACHEL DISCARDED HER GLOVES and hit the light switch beside the door. The glow from an overhead light fixture spilled down upon them. They had electricity. So far, so good.

She unzipped her parka, glad that when she left the house this morning—an eternity ago—she'd been smart enough to dress for subzero weather. This jacket might have saved her life…and Goldie's as well. She looked down at the tiny bundle she carried in the sling against her chest. The baby's eyes were closed. She wasn't moving. *Please, God, let her be all right.*

Cole hovered beside her, and she knew he was thinking the same thing.

Rachel slipped out of her jacket. Carefully, she braced the baby in her arms and adjusted the sling. *Please, God.*

Goldie's eyes popped open and she let out a wail.

Rachel had never heard a more beautiful sound. "She's okay. Yes, you are, Goldie. You're all right."

Looking up, she saw a similar relief in Cole's ruddy face. He'd torn off his cap and his hair stood up in spikes. His lips were chapped and swollen. Moisture dripped from his leather jacket. In spite of his obvious discomfort, he smiled.

Grateful tears rose behind her eyelids, but she couldn't let herself fall apart. "Are we safe?"

"I'm not sure," he said. "Tell me what Goldie needs."

The interior of the cabin was one big, open room with a couple of sofas and chairs at one end and a large wooden table at the other. The kitchen area formed an *L* shape. A closed door against the back wall probably led into the bedroom. The most important feature, in her mind, was the freestanding propane gas fireplace. "See if you can get that heater going."

She held Goldie against her shoulder, patting her back and soothing her cries. The poor little thing had to be starving. There was powdered formula in the backpack of supplies, but they needed water.

In the kitchen, Rachel turned the faucet in the sink and was rewarded with a steady flow. This simple, little cabin—probably a weekend getaway—had been well-prepared for winter. No doubt the owners had left the electricity on because the water pipes were wrapped in heat tape. The stove was electric.

Cole joined her. "The fireplace is on. What's next?"

He looked like hell. Hiking through the blizzard had been more difficult for him than for her. Not only did he go first, but his jacket and boots also weren't anywhere near as well-insulated as hers. She wanted to tell him to get out of his wet clothes, warm up and take care of himself, but she didn't want to insult his masculine pride by suggesting he wasn't in as good a shape as she was.

"Help me get stuff out of the backpack."

Near the cheery blaze in the propane fireplace, they dug through the baby supplies and put together a nest of blankets for Goldie. When Rachel laid the baby down on the blankets, her cries faded. Goldie wriggled as her diaper was changed.

Cole frowned. "Is she supposed to look like that?"

"Like what?"

"Like a plucked chicken. I thought babies were supposed to have chubby arms and legs."

"Don't listen to him." Rachel stroked Goldie's fine, dark hair. "You're gorgeous."

"Yeah, people always say that. But not all babies are beautiful."

"This is a golden child." She zipped Goldie into a yellow micro-fleece sleep sack. "She's beautiful, strong and brave—not even a day old and she's already escaped a gang of thugs and made it through a blizzard."

The baby's chin tilted, and she seemed to be looking directly at Cole with her lips pursed.

He laughed. "She's a tough little monkey."

"Newborns are surprisingly resilient." She held Goldie against her breast and stood. "I'm going to the kitchen to prepare the formula. Maybe you want to get out of those wet clothes."

"What about you?"

Her jeans were wet and cold against her legs, and her

feet were cold in spite of her lined, waterproof boots. "I'd love to take off my boots."

"Sit," he ordered.

Still holding the baby, she sank onto a rocking chair. The heat from the fireplace was making a difference in the room temperature. She couldn't allow herself to get too comfortable or she'd surely fall asleep. This had been the longest day of her life; she'd attended at two birthings, been kidnapped and escaped through a blizzard.

Cole knelt before her and unfastened the laces on her boots. He eased the boot off her right foot, cradled her heel in his hand and massaged through her wool sock. His touch felt so good that she groaned with pleasure.

"Your feet are almost dry," Cole said. "Where do I get boots like this?"

"Any outdoor clothing and equipment store." Anyone who lived in the mountains knew how to shop for snow gear. "You're not from around here."

"L.A.," he said.

This was the first bit of personal information he'd volunteered. She'd entrusted this man with her life even though she knew next to nothing about him. "What's your last name?"

"McClure." He pulled off the other boot. "And I'm not who you think I am."

Chapter Five

Rachel gazed down at the top of Cole's head as he removed her other boot. Much of his behavior didn't fit with what she expected from an armed robber. He was too smart to be a thug but dumb enough to get involved with killers. *Who is he?* In the back of her mind, she'd been waiting for the other shoe to drop. Literally, this was the moment.

He'd said that he wasn't who she thought he was. What did that mean? Did he have super powers? Was he actually a millionaire? She refused to be seduced by excuses or explanations. Rachel knew his type. He was a tough guy—dangerous, strong and silent…and sexy.

"You know what, Cole? I don't want to hear your life story."

He sat back on his heels. "Trust me. You want to know."

"Trust you?" Not wanting to upset Goldie, she kept her voice level. Inside, she was far from calm. "You don't deserve my trust."

"That's not what you said when I was saving your butt."

"I didn't ask for your help."

"Come on, Rachel. I could have left you in the middle of a shoot-out. I'm not a bad guy."

"If you hadn't hidden in the back of my van and

kidnapped me—" she paused for emphasis "—kidnapped me at gunpoint, I wouldn't have been in a shoot-out."

"There were circumstances."

"Don't care." Right now, she was supposed to be on vacation, relaxing in her cozy condo with a fragrant cup of chamomile tea and a good book. "I want this nightmare to be over. And when it is, I never want to see you again."

"Fair enough." He stood and stretched. "Take care of Goldie. I'm going to make sure we're secure."

"Go right ahead."

COLE OPENED THE CABIN DOOR and stepped onto the porch. The brief moment of warmth when he'd been inside the cabin made the cold feel even worse than before. The blizzard still raged, throwing handfuls of snow into his face. The icy temperatures instantly froze his bare hands. In his left, he held his gun. In his right, the cell phone. His intention was to call for help. Shivering, he turned on the phone. His power was almost gone. He had no signal at this remote cabin. Holding the phone like a beacon, he turned in every direction, trying to make a connection. *Nada. Damn it.* He hoped the GPS signal was still transmitting his location to his FBI handlers.

The wind-blown snow had already begun to erase their tracks. Drifts piled up, nearly two feet deep on one side of the log cabin walls. In this storm, visual surveillance was nearly impossible. He couldn't see past the trees into the forest. All he could do was try to get his bearings.

In front of the house was a turn-around driveway. Less than thirty feet away, he saw the blocky shape of a small outbuilding. A garage? There might be something in there that would aid in their escape.

The wide front door of the garage was blocked by the drifting snow, but there was a side entrance. He shoved it open and entered. The interior was unlit, but there was some illumination from a window at the rear. The open space in the middle seemed to indicate that this building was used as a garage when the people who owned the cabin were here. Under the window, he found a workbench with tools for home repair. Stacked along the walls was a variety of sporting equipment: cross-country skis, poles and snowshoes.

He'd never tried cross-country skiing before, but Rachel probably knew how to use this stuff. She was a hardy mountain woman. Prepared for the snow. Intrepid. What was her problem, anyway?

He'd been about to tell her that he was a fed and she had no more reason to fear, but she'd shut him down. Her big, beautiful blue eyes glared at him with unmistakable anger. She'd said that she didn't give a damn about him.

He didn't believe her. Though she had every reason to be ticked off, she didn't hate him. There was something growing between them. A spark. He saw it in her body language, heard it in her voice, felt it in a dim flicker inside his frozen body. Maybe after they were safe and she knew he was a good guy, he'd pursue that attraction. Or maybe not. He had a hard time imagining Rachel in sunny California, and he sure as hell wasn't going to move to these frigid, airless mountains.

Leaving the garage, he tromped along the driveway to a narrow road that hadn't been cleared of snow. No tire tracks. Nothing had been on this road since the beginning of the storm.

He looked back toward the house. Though the curtains were drawn, he could still see the light from inside. If anyone came looking for them, they wouldn't be hard to find.

CRADLING THE BABY on her shoulder, Rachel padded around in the kitchen in her wool socks. She heard the front door open and saw Cole stumble inside. He locked the door and placed his gun on the coffee table. *And his cell phone.*

"Why didn't you tell me you had a phone?" she asked.

"It's almost dead. And I can't get a signal."

Warily, she approached the table. "Who were you trying to call?"

"Somebody to get us the hell out of here."

"Like who?" She wasn't sure that she wanted to be rescued by any of his friends. *Out of the frying pan into the fire.*

"I'm not trying to trick you." He tossed the phone to her. "Go ahead. See if you can get the damn thing to work."

She juggled the phone and waved it all around while he went through the door to the bedroom. He hadn't been lying about the lack of signal, but that didn't set her mind at ease.

Returning to the kitchen, she focused on preparing the formula—a task she'd performed hundreds of times before. Not only was she the third oldest of eight children, but her responsibilities at the clinic also included more than assisting at births. She also made regular visits to new moms, helping them with baby care, feeding and providing necessary immunizations.

The water she'd put into a saucepan on the stove was just beginning to boil. Since she had no idea about the source of this liquid, she wanted to make sure germs and bacteria had been killed. Ten minutes of boiling should be enough. A cloud of steam swirled around her. From the other room, she heard doors opening and closing. She hoped Cole was changing out of his wet clothes. He looked half-frozen.

His well-being shouldn't matter to her, but she'd be lying if she told herself she wasn't attracted to him. All her life, she'd been drawn to outsiders and renegades. There was something about bad boys that always sucked her in.

Her first serious boyfriend had owned a motorcycle shop and had tattoos up and down both arms. He definitely hadn't been the kind of guy she could bring home to meet her stable, responsible, churchgoing parents, which might have been part of her fascination with him. She'd loved riding on the back of his Harley, loved the way he'd grab her and kiss her in front of his biker friends. He hadn't been able to keep his hands off her. He'd called her "baby doll" and given her a black leather jacket with a skull and a heart on the back.

On the very day she'd intended to move in with him, she'd discovered him in bed with another woman, and she'd heard him tell this leggy blond stranger that she—the blond bimbo—was his baby doll.

Even now, ten years later, that memory set Rachel's blood boiling. Before she'd departed from motorcycle man's house, she'd gone into his garage, dumped gasoline on her leather jacket and set it on fire.

After that ride on the wild side, she should have learned. Instead, she'd gone through a series of edgy boyfriends—daredevils, rock musicians, soldiers of fortune. Like an addict, she was drawn to their intensity.

Cole was one of those guys.

True, he had risked his life to rescue her and Goldie. He wasn't evil. But he wasn't somebody she wanted to know better.

Using a dish towel, she wiped around the lid of the container before she opened the powdered formula. There was food for Goldie, but what about them? Searching the kitchen, she found a supply of canned food and an opened box of crackers. There was also flour and sugar and olive oil. If they got snowed in for a day or two, they wouldn't starve to death. *A day or two?* The idea of being trapped with Cole both worried and excited her.

One-handed and still holding the fidgeting baby, she measured and mixed the formula. "Almost done," she murmured to Goldie. "You'll feel better after you eat."

One of the reasons Rachel had moved to the mountains was to get away from sexy bad boys who would ultimately hurt her. As a midwife, she didn't come into contact with many single men and hadn't had a date in months. *Fine with me!* She preferred the calm warmth of celibacy to a fiery affair that would leave her with nothing but a handful of ashes.

Bottle in hand, she returned to the living room just as Cole stepped out of the bathroom, drying his dark blond hair with a towel. He'd changed into a sweatshirt and gray sweatpants that were too short, leaving his ankles exposed. On his feet, he wore wool socks.

"Did you take a shower?" she asked.

"A hot shower. They have one of those wall-hanging propane water heaters."

She gazed longingly toward the bathroom. "Hot water?"

He held out his arms. "Give me the baby. I'll feed her while you shower and change out of those wet jeans. There are clothes in the bedroom."

That was all it took to convince her. She nodded toward the rocking chair. "Sit. Do you know how to feed an infant?"

"How hard can it be?"

"You haven't been around babies much, have you?"

"I was an only child."

Another piece of personal information she didn't need to know. "Here's how it's done. Don't force the nipple into her mouth. Let her take it. She's tired and will probably drop off before she gets enough nourishment. Gently nudge with the nipple. That stimulates the sucking reflex."

She placed Goldie in his arms and watched him. His rugged hands balanced the clear plastic bottle with a touching clumsiness. When Goldie latched onto the nipple, Cole looked up at her and grinned triumphantly. He really was trying to be helpful. She had to give him credit.

"What did you find when you went outside?" she asked. "Is it safe for us to stay here?"

"The men who were after us must have turned back. If they were still on our trail, they would have busted in here by now."

"The blizzard saved us."

"They won't stop looking. Tomorrow, we'll need to move on."

She turned on her heel and went into the bedroom. There was only one thing she needed Cole for: survival. The sooner he was out of her life, the better.

Like the rest of the cabin, the bathroom was well-equipped and efficient. Quickly, she shed her clothes and turned on the steaming water. As soon as the hot spray hit her skin, a soothing warmth spread through her body, easing her tension. She ducked her head under the hot water. One of the benefits of short hair was not worrying about getting it wet. She would have liked to stand here for hours but wasn't sure what sort of water system the cabin had. So she kept it quick.

As soon as she was out of the shower and wrapped in a yellow bath towel that matched the plastic shower curtain, Rachel realized her logistical dilemma. No way did she want to get back into her damp clothes. But she didn't want to give Cole a free show by scampering from the bathroom to the bedroom wearing nothing but a towel.

Her hand rested on the doorknob. *I can't hide in here.* Rachel prided herself on being a decisive woman. No nonsense. She did what was necessary without false modesty or complaint. And so she yanked open the bathroom door and strode forth, *decisively.* She had nothing to be ashamed of.

As she walked the few paces in her bare feet, she boldly gazed at him. In his amber eyes, she saw a flash of interest. His mouth curved in a grin.

She challenged him. "What are you staring at?"

"You."

Her bravado collapsed. She felt very, very naked. He seemed to be looking through the towel, and she had the distinct impression that he liked the view.

Despite her determination not to scamper, she dashed into the bedroom, closed the door and leaned against it. Her heart beat fast. The warmth from the shower was replaced by an internal flush of embarrassment that rose from her throat to her cheeks. If he could decimate her composure with a single glance, what would happen if he actually touched her?

In spite of the burning inside her, she realized that the temperature in the bedroom, away from the propane fireplace, was considerably cooler than in the front room. The double bed was piled high with comforters and blankets. Would she sleep in that bed with Cole tonight? As soon as the question formed in her mind, she banished it. Sleeping with the enemy had no place on her agenda.

Inside a five-drawer bureau, she found clothing—mostly long underwear and sweats—in several sizes. It was easy to imagine a family coming to this weekend retreat for cross-country skiing or ice skating or snowmobiling. When this was over, Rachel fully intended to reimburse the cabin owners and thank them for saving her life.

After she slipped into warm sweats and socks, she eyed the bedroom door. Cole was out there, waiting. Physically, she couldn't avoid him. But she could maintain an emotional distance. She remembered motorcycle man and the flaming leather jacket. Any involvement with Cole would lead inevitably to that same conclusion.

She straightened her shoulders. *I can control myself. I will control my emotions.*

She opened the door and entered the front room. Cole was still sitting in the rocking chair. Without looking up, he said, "I think Goldie's had enough milk."

"How many ounces are left in the bottle?"

He held it up to look through the clear plastic. "Just a little bit at the bottom."

"Did you burp her?"

"I do that by putting her on my shoulder, right?"

"Give me the baby," she said.

When he transferred the swaddled infant to her, their hands touched. An electric thrill raced up her arm, and she tensed her muscles to cancel the effect.

He took a step back. His baggy gray sweatsuit didn't hide the breadth of his shoulders, his slim torso or long legs. His gaze assessed her as though deciding how to proceed. Instead of speaking, he went to the front window and peered through the gap in the green-and-blue plaid curtains. "It's still snowing hard."

"This morning they predicted at least a foot of new snow." A weather report wasn't really what was on her mind.

"It's mesmerizing. I didn't actually see snow falling from the sky until I was nine years old."

"Not so pretty when you're caught in a blizzard." She did a bouncy walk as she patted Goldie on the back.

"I never want to do that again."

"Tomorrow morning, we shouldn't have to walk too far. All we need to find is a working telephone."

Then they could call for help. She and Goldie would be safe. Cole was a different story. When the police came to her rescue, he'd be taken into custody. Would he turn himself in without a fight? Or would he run?

"It's ironic," he said. "This is the first time in years that I've been without a working cell phone."

Had he planned it that way? She needed to clear the air of suspicions. "Cole, I—"

A shuffling sound outside the front door interrupted her, and she turned to look in that direction.

The door crashed open. A hulking figure charged across the threshold. His shoulders and cap were covered with snow. His lips drew back from his teeth in an inhuman snarl.

He had a gun.

Chapter Six

Frank Loeb! Cole barely recognized him. The man should have been dead. He'd been shot. Cole had seen his blood spattered in the snow. How the hell had he made it through the blizzard? Some men were just too damned mean to die.

Frank raised his handgun.

Cole's weapon was all the way across the room on the table. No time to grab it. No chance for subtlety or reason. He launched himself at the monster standing in the doorway. His shoulder drove into the other man's massive chest.

With a guttural yell, Frank staggered backward onto the porch. He was off balance, weakened. Cole pressed his advantage. He shoved with all his strength. His hands slipped against the cold, wet, bloodstained parka. The big man teetered and fell. Cole was on top of him. He slammed Frank's gun hand on the floor of the porch.

Frank released his grasp on the gun. He was disarmed but still dangerous. Flailing, he landed heavy blows on Cole's arms and shoulders. The snow gusted around them. Icy crystals hit Cole's face, stinging like needles.

He drew back his fist and slammed it into Frank's face, splitting his swollen lip. He winced. Blood oozed down his chin.

Cole hit him again. His fingers stung with the force of the blow.

"Wait." Frank lay still. The fight went out of him.

With his arm still cocked for another blow, Cole paused. He knew better than to let down his guard. He'd seen Frank in action. When the big man caught one of the other guys in the gang cheating at cards, Frank broke two of the cheater's fingers. And he smiled at the pain he had inflicted.

"The shooters," Frank said. "They were feds."

That wasn't possible. Though Cole had put in a call for backup, the shooters had appeared within minutes. Even if the FBI had been tracking his movements, the violent assault on the house wasn't standard procedure, especially not when they had a man on the inside. "I don't believe it."

"They were after you." His tongue poked at his split lip. "I heard them talking. They said your name."

"What else did you hear?"

"They reported to somebody named Prescott."

Wayne Prescott was the field agent in charge of the Denver office—the only individual Cole had met with in person. "How did you find us?"

His eyes squeezed shut. Clearly, he was in pain. "Wasn't looking for you."

"The hell you weren't."

"On the run. Just like you," he mumbled. "Went across a field. Saw the lights from the cabin."

Rachel stepped out on the porch. She took a shooter's stance, holding his gun in both hands and aiming at Frank. "Don't move. I will shoot."

There was no doubt that she meant what she'd said. Her voice was firm and her hand steady. She positioned herself far enough away from Frank that he couldn't make a grab for her ankle.

"You're a medic," Frank said. "I need your help."

Cole noticed a flicker of doubt in her eyes. Her natural instinct was to save lives, not threaten them. Even though he wasn't inclined to help Frank, he couldn't justify killing the man in cold blood.

He stood, picked up Frank's gun and aimed for the center of his chest. "Get up."

Moving slowly and laboriously, Frank got to his knees. Then he heaved himself to his feet and stood there with blood dripping down his chin onto his wet black parka.

Cole instructed, "Rachel, go inside. Keep your distance from him. If he makes a move toward you, shoot him."

After she was safely in the house, Cole escorted his prisoner into the cabin. He saw Goldie sleeping, nestled in blankets on one of the sofas. He had to protect that innocent baby. If Frank wasn't lying, Cole's hope for a rescue from the FBI was disintegrating fast. Agent Wayne Prescott was connected with the men who opened fire on the house. *Houston, we have a problem.*

With the gun, he gestured toward the bedroom. "In there."

Rachel wasted no time closing the front door. Frank had broken the latch, and she had to pull a chair in front of it to keep it shut.

In the bedroom, Cole ordered, "Take off the parka."

Frank peeled off his jacket. A swath of gore stained the left side of his plaid flannel shirt and the left arm. It looked like he'd been shot twice. It was a miracle that he'd made it this far.

The question was whether or not to treat his wounds. They didn't have medical supplies, but Rachel could probably do something for him. Cole hated the idea of her getting close to this dangerous criminal.

Frank groaned. "You had me fooled, man. I thought you were just some punk from Compton. But you've got the feds on your tail. You must have pulled something big-time."

Cole was aware of Rachel standing behind him, listening. He glanced toward her. "Find something to tie his hands and feet."

"We need to clean those wounds," she said. "He could still be losing blood."

"Listen to her," Frank said. "I don't want to die."

"Why should I help you? You crashed through the door with a gun."

"But I didn't shoot."

A valid point. Frank had caught them unawares but hadn't opened fire. What did he want from them?

Cole asked Rachel, "How would you treat him?"

"He needs to go into the bathroom, strip down and get out of his wet clothes. Then he should clean his wounds with soap. Once I can see the extent of the damage, I'll tell you what else is necessary."

"I still want you to find something to tie him up." He turned back to Frank. "Here's the deal. Do exactly as she says, and I won't kill you."

He nodded. This willingness to cooperate was out of character. Maybe he was intimidated by his new idea of Cole's reputation. Maybe the loss of blood had weakened him.

Cole stood in the bathroom door and watched as the big man sat on the toilet seat and pulled off his boots, socks and wet jeans. His skin was raw. His feet had white streaks, indicating the start of frostbite, but the more serious physical problem became evident when he removed his shirt. Blood caked and congealed on his upper chest and left arm. When he turned his back, Cole didn't see an exit wound.

"You need treatment in a hospital," Cole said. "The bullet is still in your chest."

"I'm not going back to prison."

"Jail is better than a coffin."

"Not for me."

After Frank had pulled on a pair of sweatpants and dry socks, he washed the wounds. His left arm wasn't too bad, but the hole in his upper chest was ragged at the edges and slowly bleeding. It had to hurt like hellfire. Cole had never been shot, but he'd nursed a knife wound for three hours without treatment.

Still holding his gun, he tossed Frank a towel. "Press this against your chest, and come into the kitchen."

Frank shuffled forward obediently. His heavy shoulders slouched. His head drooped forward, and his long hair hung around his face in strings. He reminded Cole of an injured grizzly, willing to accept help but still capable of lethal violence.

After he was seated in a straight-back chair, Rachel went into the bathroom to look for first-aid supplies.

"How did you get away?" Cole asked.

"I lay still, played possum. They thought I was dead. When they all went inside, I got up and ran. Two of them went after you and Rachel. They had flashlights."

"You were following them?"

"I was going parallel up the slope behind the house. I thought for sure they'd hear me."

The wind and the fury of the oncoming blizzard had masked the sounds from desperate people climbing through the forest. "You had a gun."

"Nothing like the kind of heat they were packing. Damn feds. They've got the primo weapons."

Not always. "When did they turn back?"

"Didn't even make it to the top of the hill." Frank grimaced. "I kept going. Picked up your trail. Then I got to an open field. The snow was coming down hard. Couldn't see a damn thing. Man, I thought I was going to die out there in the field. Frozen stiff." He barked a laugh. "A stiff. Frozen. Get it?"

Rachel returned with an armful of supplies, which she placed on the table. "I found antiseptic, gauze and surgical tape. I think I can make this work."

When she approached Frank and touched his shoulder, Cole's gut clenched. Though she showed no sign of fear, he knew how dangerous Frank could be. If the big man took it into his head to attack her, Cole couldn't risk shooting him. Not while Rachel was so close. He holstered his gun and took a position behind Frank's right shoulder, preparing himself to react to any threatening move.

Focused on first aid, Rachel lightly probed the wound on Frank's chest.

He inhaled sharply. The muscles in his chest twitched. "What are you doing?"

"Feeling for the bullet," she said. "I'm afraid it's deeply embedded."

"Cut it out of me."

"That's a painful process, and we've got no anesthetic. Not even booze. Plus, you've already lost a lot of blood. If I open that wound wider, you could bleed to death."

"I can take the pain," Frank said.

"But I can't give you a transfusion. For now, I'm going to patch you up and get the bleeding stopped. Later, you can deal with surgical procedures."

"Just do it."

Quickly and efficiently, she dressed the wound on his arm and wrapped it with strips of cotton from a T-shirt she'd shredded. "We're going to owe the people who own this cabin a whole new wardrobe," she said. "All this stuff is saving our lives."

"But no booze," Frank muttered.

She peeled the wrapper off a tampon and removed it from the casing. "I'm going to use this to plug the hole in your chest. It's sterile. And the absorbency will stop the bleeding."

Cole had heard of using feminine products to staunch blood flow but had never seen it done. Frank would owe his life to a tampon. Cole kept himself from smirking.

Frank turned his head away as she packed the wound. "You got to be pretty good friends with Penny," he said.

"We talked." A frown pulled Rachel's mouth.

"What did you talk about?"

"Anything that would take her mind off the labor pains," Rachel said. "Her childhood. Her dreams."

"Her baby's daddy? Baron?"

"I know you guys work for him and think he's a big deal, but I think he's a jerk. Sending his pregnant girlfriend to rob a casino?" She finished taping and wrapping the wound. "What kind of man does something like that?"

Frank's right hand shot forward. He held Rachel's jaw in his grip and pulled her face close to his. "Where did Penny hide the money?"

Cole reacted. He broke Frank's grasp and yanked his arm behind his back. The damage had already been done.

When he looked at Rachel, he saw fear written all over

her face. Frank had achieved his objective. He'd showed her that he was someone who would hurt her if she didn't do as he said. Cole hadn't protected her; she'd never trust him now.

Chapter Seven

After checking one more time to make sure Goldie was sleeping peacefully, Rachel sat at the end of the long table in the cabin. She slouched, head bent forward. With her fingernail, she traced the grain of the wood on the tabletop. The unidentifiable aroma of something Cole was cooking on the stove assaulted her nostrils.

Though she tried to focus on simple things, Rachel couldn't dismiss her rising fears. When Frank grabbed her, she hadn't been bruised. But she could still feel the imprint of his fingers. His grip had been ferocious—strong as a vise squeezing her jawbone. He could have killed her. With a flick of his wrist, he could have broken her neck. He'd forced her to look into his dark, soulless eyes. His split lip had sneered when he asked where Penny hid the money.

She hadn't expected the big man to lash out. Not while she was helping him by dressing his wounds. Her mistake had been letting down her guard and getting too close to him. The warmth of the cabin had imbued her with false feelings of security.

She wasn't safe. Not by a long shot.

Trusting Cole was out of the question. His subtle charm was more potentially devastating than a blatant assault. She'd heard Frank say that the FBI was chasing Cole.

Those men with guns who came to the house had been after Cole.

He placed a bowl of the canned chili he'd been heating in front of her. Though she should have been starving, Rachel didn't have an appetite. As she picked a kidney bean from the chili with her spoon, she felt Cole watching her.

"You don't have to worry about Frank," he said. "I've got him tied down in the bedroom."

Though Frank scared the hell out of her, she didn't want to mistreat him. "He should eat something."

"I'm not going to feed him. He'd probably bite my hand off. Besides, he's fallen asleep."

"Or gone into a coma," she said.

"I don't want him to die," Cole said. "I wouldn't wish death on anyone. But I've done all I intend to do for Frank Loeb."

At least he was being honest. She dared to lift her gaze from the chili and look into his face. His cognac-colored eyes gleamed. The color had returned to his roughly stubbled cheeks. It wasn't fair for him to be so handsome. The evil he might have done wasn't apparent in his features.

She shoveled a bite of chili into her mouth. The taste was bland and the texture gooey, but she swallowed and took another bite. If she was going to survive, she needed her strength.

Cole said, "Not the world's best dinner. Would you like a stale cracker to go with it?"

She shook her head, not wanting to get into a conversation with him. Given half a chance, he'd seduce her with his smooth-talking lies.

"You might be wondering," he said, "about some of the things Frank said."

"Not at all." She forced herself to swallow more chili.

"There are a couple of things you need to know, starting with—"

"Stop." She held up her hand. "I don't want to hear it."

"Five words," he said. "Give me five words to explain myself."

"All right. And I'm counting."

"I'm. An. Undercover. FBI. Agent." He shrugged. "Maybe FBI ought to count as more than one word. But you get the idea."

She dropped her spoon. *I didn't see this coming.* "Why should I believe you?"

He grinned. "Are you willing to hear more?"

Not if he was lying. "I want the truth."

"Until tomorrow when we talk to the police, I can't prove my identity," he said. "The mere fact that I'm willing to turn myself in to the cops ought to tell you something. My handler works out of the Denver field office. I contacted him after the shoot-out at the casino, and he told me to stick with the gang."

"Even though Penny was wounded and pregnant?"

"I thought the gang would make a clean getaway. She seemed okay. And I didn't expect her to go into labor."

"But she did. Wasn't it your duty to protect her and her baby?"

"That's why I got you."

"And put me in danger." If he really was an undercover agent, he was utterly irresponsible. "A real FBI agent wouldn't put a civilian in harm's way."

"Think back," he said. "I was doing my best to keep you safe. I kept you from seeing the other members of the gang so they wouldn't think you could identify them. Damn it, Rachel. Before the shoot-out started, I was taking you to your van, helping you escape."

Some of what he was saying backed up his claim to be an undercover lawman, but all she could see when she looked back was Penny, lying dead on the floor after delivering her baby. "She didn't deserve to die."

"I never thought Penny would be harmed. She was the mother of Baron's child. That should have been a guarantee of safety." His smile had disappeared. "But you're right, Rachel. Her death—her murder—was my fault. I failed. I can tell myself that there was nothing I could have done to save her, but it doesn't change what happened. Somehow, I'll have to find a way to live with that."

His regret seemed real. Did she dare to believe him? From the start, she'd sensed that he was a dangerous man. As an undercover agent, that was true. Even if he was on the right side of the law, he had that renegade edge. "Why didn't you tell me before? We were alone in my van when you kidnapped me. You could have told me then."

"If you'd known I was undercover, you would have been in even more danger."

Again, his reasoning made sense. But she couldn't allow herself to be drawn in to this improbable story. "Frank said the FBI was after you. Not the other way around."

"And that could be a big problem." He glanced toward the closed door to the bedroom where Frank lay unconscious. "Usually, I'd dismiss anything Frank said as a lie, but he came up with a name that makes me think twice."

"I'm listening."

"Let me start at the beginning." Ignoring his chili, he leaned back in his chair and stretched his long legs out in front of him. "It was a month ago, give or take a couple of days. The FBI had an opportunity to infiltrate Baron's operation. They recruited me from L.A. because they suspected there was an FBI agent working with Baron. None of the agents in the Rocky Mountain area know me."

"Except for your handler."

"His name is Wayne Prescott. That's the name Frank heard. One of the shooters at the house mentioned Prescott."

"The shooters were from the FBI?"

"I don't think so. Attacking the house with guns blazing isn't the way we do things, especially not when the shooters knew they had an agent on the inside. Before they opened fire, they would have negotiated and offered a chance to surrender."

"Is that always the way they work?"

"In my experience, yes."

His gaze was steadfast and unguarded. His posture, relaxed. He didn't seem to be lying, but an expert liar wouldn't show that he was nervous. "Well, then. How do you explain what happened at the house?"

"The shooters know Prescott, but they have to be Baron's men. Penny told us that he owned the cabin and knew the location. Baron has a reputation for cruelty. During the casino robbery, our gang screwed up by getting into a shoot-out and attracting attention. My guess is that he wanted us all dead rather than in custody."

"All of you? Even the mother of his child?"

"I've been undercover a lot, and I still don't understand the criminal mind. A lot of these guys seem perfectly normal. They have wives and kids. They live in houses in the suburbs and drive hybrids. But they don't think the same way that we do. They don't follow the same ideas of morality. Baron might have a moment of sadness about Penny and Goldie, but he won't let their death stop his master plan."

"Even if he loved her?"

"A guy like that?" Cole leaned forward, picked up his spoon and dug into the chili. "He's not capable of love."

Penny had certainly thought differently. During the time she was in labor, she'd talked about her relationship with Goldie's father. They'd known each other since she was a teenager. Not that they were the typical hand-holding high school sweethearts. Baron was older than she was—much older. The way they'd met wasn't clear to Rachel, but he was somehow connected to her high school.

Penny had talked about the way he swept her off her feet. He drove an expensive car and gave her presents and took her to classy restaurants.

The thought of this older man taking advantage of Penny disgusted Rachel, but she'd kept her opinion to herself. When a woman was in the midst of labor, she didn't need to have a serious relationship discussion.

She asked, "Why did Frank think I knew where Penny hid the money?"

"Do you?"

"She mentioned the hidden cash. It was her insurance policy to make sure the gang wouldn't kill her. But she never said where it was, and I didn't really know what she was talking about."

"It's complicated," he said.

"Explain it." She leaned back in her chair. "We've got time."

Cole took one more bite of chili before he responded. "Baron runs five gangs—maybe more—throughout the Rocky Mountain region. He does the prep work—figures out the site of each robbery and the timing. The gang goes in, makes the grab and gets away fast."

"Always at casinos?"

"Usually not. Casinos generally have better security than banks. The typical target is a small bank. The heists are nothing clever. Just get in and get out. Then comes the genius part of Baron's scheme."

In spite of her skepticism, she found herself being drawn into his story. "How is it genius?"

"A lot of robbers get caught when they start to spend the money. Sometimes, it's marked. Passing off hundred-dollar bills isn't easy. And the robbers can't exactly take their haul and deposit it in a regular bank account."

"Why not?"

"Think about it," he said. "If somebody like Frank strolls into a bank and wants to open an account with hundred-dollar bills, a bank teller is going to get suspicious."

She nodded. "I see what you mean."

"Baron has a designated person—in our gang, it was Penny—who puts the cash into a package and mails it to a secure location."

"What do you mean by secure location?" she asked. "It seems like Baron would want the money sent directly to him."

"But that would mean that his location could be traced."

"Okay, I get it," she said. "Then what?"

"After a couple of weeks when the heat is off, the designated person either picks up the money and hand delivers it. Or they give Baron the location and he arranges for a pickup. He launders the cash and keeps half. The gang gets paid a monthly stipend, just like a real job."

She could see why the FBI wanted to shut down Baron's operation. "How much money are we talking about?"

"Five gangs pulling off two or three jobs a month. The take ranges from a couple thousand to twenty. I figure it's more than a hundred thousand a month."

"I can't believe all these gangs keep getting away with it," she said.

"You'd be surprised how many bank robberies there are," he said. "Last year in Colorado alone, there were over a hundred and fifty. Most of the time, they don't even make the news. Especially when there's not a huge amount of cash involved and no one is injured."

She finished off her chili while she considered what he'd told her. Baron's scheme sounded far too complicated for Cole to have made it up, but that still didn't prove that he was working undercover for the FBI.

His behavior while she'd been held captive was more convincing. During the whole time Penny was in labor, he'd been a gentleman. Like he said, he'd kept her separate from the other gang members. And he had been helping her escape when the shooters attacked.

She shivered from a draft that slipped around the edge of the front door. Though they'd pushed a chair against it and blocked the air with towels from the bathroom, the door didn't fit exactly into the frame after Frank burst through it.

Rising from the table, she carried her bowl to the kitchen and looked out the uncurtained window. "Still snowing."

"That's a good thing." He reached around her to put his bowl in the sink. "The blizzard will keep anybody from searching for us."

Though they weren't alone in the cabin, she felt as if they were sharing a private moment in the kitchen. Outside the wind rushed and hurled icy pellets at the window, but they were tucked away and sheltered.

When she turned toward him, he didn't back away. Less than two feet of space separated them. "Why did you tell me all this?"

"I wanted you to know. I'm one of the good guys, and I'm not going to hurt you."

She'd heard that promise before. Other men had assured her that they wouldn't break her heart. The smart thing would be to step away, to put some distance between them. But they were awfully close. And he was awfully good-looking.

Arms folded below her breasts, she tried to shut down her attraction to him. Diffidently, she asked, "Why do you care what I think?"

"I like you, Rachel."

He could have said so much more, could have called her his baby doll and told her she was beautiful. "Is that all you have to say?"

"I like you…very much."

And she liked him, too. In spite of her resolution to steer clear of dangerous men, she unfolded her arms. Gently, she reached up and rested her hand on his cheek. His stubble bristled under her fingers. Electricity crackled between them.

His hand clasped her waist as his head lowered. His lips were firm. He used exactly the right amount of pressure for a perfect kiss.

She pulled away from him and opened her eyes. His smile was warm. His eyes, inviting. *Perfect! Of course!* Guys like Cole—men who lived on the edge—made the best lovers. Because they didn't hold back? Because they took risks in everything?

"That was good," she said.

"I can do better."

He stepped forward, trapping her against the kitchen counter, and encircled her in a powerful embrace. Through the bulky sweatsuits, their bodies joined. This kiss was harder and more demanding. If she allowed herself to respond, she didn't know if she could stop. In minutes, she'd be tearing off his clothes and dragging him onto her and…

His tongue slid into her mouth, and her mind went blank. Sensation washed through her, sending an army of goose bumps marching along the surface of her skin. She felt so good, so alive. Though she was unaware of moving a muscle, her back arched. Her breasts pressed against his chest, and the sensitive tips of her nipples tingled with pleasure. Her feet seemed to leave the floor as though she was weightless. Floating. Drifting through clouds.

When the kiss ended, she lightly descended to earth. *Oh, man, that was some kiss!* A rocket to the moon.

Still holding her, he leaned back and gazed down at her. She stared up at his face, watching as his lips pulled into a confident smile. He knew his kiss had affected her. He knew that he was in control.

In spite of her dazed state, Rachel realized that she needed to pull back. She'd have to be crazy to make love to him tonight. It wasn't possible. Not with baby Goldie sleeping nearby. Not with psychopathic Frank tied up in the bedroom.

She couldn't manage a single coherent word, but he must have sensed her reticence because he loosened his grasp and stepped back.

"I want to make love to you, Rachel." His voice was low and rough. "I want you. Now."

"Uh-huh."

"But the time isn't right."

She nodded so vigorously that she made herself dizzy. "Not tonight."

"You're a special woman. I want to treat you right."

"Uh-huh."

"And I want you to trust me."

"Okay."

He took her hand and squeezed. "When we're safe and this is over," he said with the sexiest smile she'd ever seen. "It won't be over between you and me. That's a promise."

Chapter Eight

After Cole converted one of the sofas into a double bed and got Rachel and Goldie settled down to sleep, he stretched out on the other sofa on the opposite side of the cabin. Between his side of the front room and Rachel's the gas fireplace blazed warmly. His gun rested on the floor beside him, easily reachable. Though the sofa was too short for his legs, this wasn't the worst place he'd gone to bed. His undercover work meant he sometimes didn't know where he'd be sleeping or for how long.

Over the years, he'd trained himself to drop easily into a light slumber. Never a deep sleep. Not while on assignment. Even while resting, he needed to maintain vigilance, to be prepared for the unexpected threat.

As soon as he closed his eyes, he became aware of aching muscles from their hike and bruises from his fight with Frank. Ignoring the pain, he concentrated on letting go of his tension, keeping his breathing steady and lowering his pulse rate.

He tried to imagine a blank slate. Soft blue. Peaceful. But his mind raced, jumping from one visual image to another. He saw Penny in a pool of her own blood. Saw Frank being gunned down, throwing his arms into the air before he fell. He saw snow swirling before his eyes. Then through the whiteness, Rachel's face emerged. Her startling blue eyes opened wide. He saw Goldie in Rachel's arms. The baby reached toward him with her tiny hands.

No matter what else happened, he had to make sure Goldie and Rachel got to a safe place—a task that should have been easy. He should have been able to make one phone call and rest assured that the FBI would swoop in for a rescue. But he was wary of his connections, and he'd learned to trust his instincts. If he smelled trouble, there was usually something rotten. Special Agent Wayne Prescott?

Cole had only met with Prescott once at a hotel in Grand Junction for a briefing before his assignment. Though dressed in casual jeans and a parka, Agent Prescott had presented himself as a buttoned-down professional with neatly barbered brown hair and a clean-shaven chin. An administrator. A desk jockey. He had passed on the necessary information in a businesslike manner.

Cole had refused his offer of a cell phone with local numbers already programmed in. By keeping his own cell phone, Cole had more autonomy. Not only did his private directory have phone numbers for people he trusted, but his phone also had the capability of disabling the GPS locator so he couldn't be found.

Though his handlers didn't agree, Cole found it necessary at times to be completely off the grid. His current situation was a good example. If Prescott could track his location, they might be in even more danger.

Cole's eyelids snapped open. Though his body was exhausted, his mind was too busy for sleep.

Leaving the sofa, he went toward the kitchen table where he'd left his phone. Shortly after Frank mentioned Prescott's name, Cole had turned off the GPS. But was it really off? His boss in L.A., Agent Waxman, hadn't been pleased about having his undercover agent untraceable.

Had Waxman programmed in some kind of tracking mechanism?

If Frank had been awake and hadn't been a psycho, Cole would have turned to him for help in analyzing his phone's capabilities. Frank had expert skills with electronics.

For a moment, Cole toyed with the idea of destroying his cell phone. Then he decided against it. Tomorrow when the blizzard lifted, they could use his phone to call for help. *Yeah? And who would he call? Who could he trust?*

Through the kitchen window—the only one without a curtain—he saw the snow continue to fall. His visibility was limited. He couldn't tell if it was letting up—not that it mattered. There was nothing they could do tonight. Trying to fight their way through the blizzard and the drifts in the dark would be suicide. They had to wait until morning. Until then, he needed to sleep, damn it. His body required a couple of hours' solid rest to replenish his physical resources.

He headed back toward his sofa but found himself standing over Rachel. She lay on her back, covered up to her chin with a plaid wool blanket. The light from the gas fireplace flickered across her cheeks and smooth forehead. Her full lips parted slightly, and her breathing was steady.

Hers was an unassuming beauty. No makeup. No frills. No nonsense. Her thick, black lashes were natural, as were her dark eyebrows that matched the wisps of hair framing her face.

Looking down, he realized that she was the real reason he couldn't sleep. He'd made her a promise, told her that they'd have a relationship beyond this ordeal. That was what he wanted. To spend time with her. To learn more about this complicated woman whose livelihood was bringing new life into the world.

He admired her strength of character and wondered what caused her defensiveness. Until she had melted into his arms, she'd been pushing him away with both hands. But she'd kissed him with passion and yearning. No way had that kiss been a timid testing of the waters. She'd committed herself. She'd responded as though she'd been waiting for him to strike a spark and ignite the flame.

He reached toward her but didn't actually touch her cheek. He didn't want to wake her; she needed her sleep. *I didn't lie to you, Rachel.*

But he hadn't been completely honest. A man in his line of work changed his identity the way other people changed their socks. He never knew how long he'd be on assignment and unable to communicate with a significant other. Bottom line: he couldn't commit to a real, in-depth relationship.

Tearing his gaze away from her, he went back to his sofa and lay down. This time, he fell asleep.

It seemed like only a few minutes later that he heard Goldie's cries. He bolted upright on the sofa. His gun was in his hand.

Rachel was already awake. "It's okay," she said. "Don't shoot."

After a quick scan of the cabin, he lowered his weapon. "What's wrong with her?"

"She's hungry." Rachel opened the blanket she used to swaddle the infant and picked her up. Immediately—as if by magic—the wailing stopped. Rachel bent her head down to nuzzle Goldie's tummy. "Most babies wake up a couple of times at night."

He knew that. A long time ago, he had a female partner with a newborn baby boy. She was always complaining about not getting enough sleep. "Anything I can do to help?"

"I'll handle this."

She got no argument from him. Through half-closed eyes, he watched her taking care of the baby. Her movements were efficient but exceedingly gentle as she changed the diaper. Even though Goldie wasn't hers, it was obvious that Rachel cared deeply for this infant. He understood; babies were pretty damned lovable.

As she walked to the kitchen she bounced with each step and made soft, cooing sounds. Her voice soothed him. So sweet. So tender. He closed his eyes and imagined her lying beside him, humming and—

"Cole." Frank's shout tore him out of his reverie. "Damn you, Cole. Get in here."

Cole groaned. He would have much preferred changing diapers to dealing with a wounded psychopath. With his gun in hand, he crossed the room and shoved open the bedroom door. In this room away from the fireplace, the temperature was about ten degrees cooler and it was dark. Cole turned on the overhead light. "What?"

"Untie me. I've got to pee."

The restraints Cole had used on Frank were a combination of twine, rope and bungee cords. There was enough play in the ropes that fastened his wrists to the bed frame on either side of him that he could get comfortable. The same went for his ankles, which were attached to the iron frame at the foot of the bed. Setting him free involved a certain amount of risk. Frank could turn on him; he needed to be handled with extreme caution.

Cole was tired of dealing with men like Frank. Always trying to stay two steps ahead. Never letting his guard down. He didn't like what his life had become.

He came closer to the bed and unzipped the sweatshirt stretched across his chest. The wound near his shoulder showed only a light bloodstain. Rachel's tampon plug had done its job in stopping the bleeding.

"Here's the deal, Frank. If you give me any trouble, I'll shoot. No hesitation. No second thoughts. Understand?"

"Yeah, yeah, I get it."

One-handed, he unfastened the cords. All the while, he kept his weapon trained on the big man. Once he was free, Frank stretched his arms and winced in pain. He hauled his legs to the edge of the bed. Slowly, he lumbered to the bathroom, where Cole stood watch. Not a pleasant experience for either of them.

When they returned to the bedroom, Frank sat on the bed and reached for the water glass on the bedside table. He swallowed a few gulps and licked his lips. "I'm hungry."

"Too bad."

"You don't have to tie me up, man. I'm not going to—"

"Save it." Cole wasn't taking any chances. Not with Rachel and Goldie in the other room.

With his finger, Frank touched his split lip. "As soon as the snow stops, we should move on. Those feds are still after you."

"Lie down. Arms at your sides. Legs straight."

"You need me. When those guys catch up to you, you're going to want somebody watching your back. Come on, man. I'm a good person to have on your side in a fight. You know that."

There were a few things Cole knew for certain. The first was that Frank enjoyed inflicting pain. The second, he was a bully who couldn't be trusted. Number three, he was smarter than he looked. "You can lie down. Now. Or I'll knock you unconscious. Your choice."

With a low growl, Frank stretched out on the bed. "I've

been lying here, thinking. I know what you're up to. You've got leverage. A couple of bargaining chips."

Cole fastened the cords on his ankles. "You just keep thinking, Frank."

"You're going to use the baby to deal with Baron. I mean, Baron is as mean as they come, but he's not going to kill his own kid, right?"

While Cole dealt with the bonds on Frank's wrists, he pressed the nose of his gun into the big man's belly.

"And Rachel," Frank said. "She's going to take you to where Penny sent the loot. Oh, yeah, I got it all figured out. But there's something you don't know."

"What's that?" Cole finished securing the ropes and stepped back. "What don't I know?"

"If I tell you, I'm giving up my own bargaining chip."

As far as Cole was concerned, Frank could keep his information to himself. Tomorrow, after he and Rachel were far away from this cabin, he'd call the local police and give them the location. The cops could take Frank into custody.

Cole turned toward the door.

"Hey," Frank called after him. "I can tell you why the feds attacked. You want to know that, don't you?"

Clearly, Frank was grasping at straws, trying to play him. In other circumstances, Cole might have been interested in his information, but he was weary of these games. "Whether you tell me or not, I don't give a damn."

He wanted to get back to a semblance of normal life, to take Rachel home to California with him and show her his favorite beach. He hadn't seen much of her body, except when she stepped out of the bathroom in a towel, but he thought she'd look good in a bikini.

"It's about the money," Frank said. "Penny told me that she was keeping the place she'd sent the last three packages a secret from Baron. That's got to be close to seventy thousand bucks. Just sitting there. Waiting to be picked up."

"I don't believe you. Penny wouldn't try a double cross on Baron."

"She said that she wasn't going to steal from him. She just wanted to see him. And she knew he'd come for the money."

Though the idea disgusted him, Cole understood Penny's reasoning. Baron wouldn't come to see his pregnant girlfriend or his newborn child. But he'd make an effort for the money. "So what?"

"I'm betting Rachel knows where it is. She and Penny were getting real chummy." He gave a grotesque wink. "We can make her tell us where the money is hidden."

"Go back to sleep."

He closed the bedroom door and stepped into the front room, where Rachel sat in the rocking chair feeding Goldie by the golden light from the gas fireplace. Cole felt as if he'd entered a different world. A better place, for sure. The energy in this room nurtured him and gave him hope.

When Rachel met his gaze and smiled, he wanted to gather her into his arms and hold her close. He needed her honesty and decency. She was the antidote to the ugly life he'd been living.

"How is Frank doing?" she asked.

"I checked the wound. There's very little bleeding."

"He needs to get to a hospital tomorrow."

He wanted to tell her that tomorrow would bring a solution to all their problems. But he couldn't make that promise.

IN THE DIM LIGHT OF DAWN, Rachel stepped onto the porch of the cabin and shivered. The furry bristles of her parka hood froze instantly and scraped against her cheek as she adjusted Goldie's position inside the sling carrier under her parka.

The blizzard had dwindled to a sputtering of snow, but the skies were still blanketed with heavy gray clouds. Cole joined her on the porch and held up his cell phone.

"Still no signal," he said.

"We shouldn't have to go too far." She pointed with her gloved hand toward a break in the trees. "It looks like a road up there. There ought to be other cabins. We should be able to find somebody with a working phone."

From inside the cabin, Frank yelled out a curse at Cole and threatened revenge. His voice was hoarse and rasping. She knew they couldn't trust Frank but felt guilty for leaving him tied to the bed.

As Cole fastened the broken front door closed with a bungee cord, she asked, "We're going to get help for Frank, aren't we?"

"When we talk to the cops, we'll give them the location of this cabin. Frank won't be happy about being rescued and arrested at the same time."

"I almost feel sorry for him."

"Don't."

Before they'd left the cabin, she'd made a final check on Frank's wounds. The bleeding had stopped, and he wasn't in imminent danger. Though the cabin wasn't cold, he'd told her that he was freezing and asked her to cover him up with his parka. She figured it was the least she could do for him.

She fell into step behind Cole. The oversized backpack on his shoulders blocked the wind. Though this area had been sheltered from the full force of the storm by trees, the new-fallen snow was well over her boots—probably a foot deep. On the north side of the cabin, the drifts reached all the way to the windowsill.

Cole led the way to a log structure that looked like a garage. He shoved the door open and ushered her inside.

"Which do you prefer?" he asked. "Cross-country skis or snowshoes?"

"What are you thinking?" He claimed to be one of the good guys but he acted like a thief. "We can't just walk in here and help ourselves. We've already destroyed the front door on the cabin, made a mess and eaten their food."

"Don't worry. It hasn't escaped my attention that this well-equipped little cabin saved our lives. I fully intend to pay the owners back."

"Did you leave a note?"

"It kind of defeats the purpose of being undercover if I start handing out my address."

"How about money?" she demanded. "Did you leave cash?"

"I'm sending people back here for Frank. If I left cash, somebody else would pick it up. Don't worry, I'll pay for the damages."

In an unconscious gesture, he patted the left side of his jacket then pulled his hand away. She was beginning to understand the sneaky undercover side to his personality. Every twitch had a meaning. She asked, "What's in your pocket? Are you hiding something from me?"

"Do you have to know everything?"

"Yes."

"Fine," he said. "I've got nothing in my pocket, but there's a pouch with cash, a switchblade and a new identity sewn into the lining."

"Impressive."

"In spite of this disaster, I'm good at my job. The hardest part of an undercover op is getting out in one piece." He sorted through the array of skis and snowshoes. "What's best for moving through the snow?"

She still didn't want to steal the equipment. If somebody took her cross-country skis, she'd be furious. "Why can't we just hike up to the road? Even if it hasn't been cleared recently, the snowplows will be coming through."

"We aren't taking the road."

"Why not?"

He held a set of snowshoes toward her. "The shooters—whether they're FBI or Baron's men—are going to be looking for us."

His gaze met hers. Even in the dark garage, she could see his tension. If they were found, they'd be killed. Normal rules of conduct didn't apply. She pulled off her gloves and took the snowshoes.

Chapter Nine

After a bit of trial and error, Cole figured out how to walk in the snowshoes with minimal tripping over his own feet. Even using the ski poles for balance, he'd fallen twice.

From behind his back, Rachel called out, "You're getting the hang of it. Don't try to go backwards."

He muttered, "It's like I've got tennis rackets strapped to my shoes."

"That's still better than plowing through two feet of new snow."

Or not. The winter sports he enjoyed involved speed—racing across open terrain on a snowmobile, streaking down a slope on downhill skis or a snowboard. A clumsy slog through deep snow was the opposite of fun—another reason to hate Colorado. After last night's blizzard, he'd lost any appreciation he might have had for the scenic beauty of a winter wonderland. All this pristine whiteness depressed the hell out of him. Never again would he take an undercover assignment in the mountains. A tropical jungle filled with snakes and man-eating lions would be preferable.

Though they weren't on the road, he stayed on a trail through the forest that ran parallel to it. The worst thing that could happen now was to get lost in this unpopulated back country. They'd been hiking on snowshoes for nearly half an hour—long enough for him to freeze the tip of his nose—and they still hadn't sighted a cabin.

The dawn light was beginning to brighten, and the snowfall lacked the fury of the blizzard. On the opposite side of the road, he could see the outline of a tall ridge through the icy mist. What lay beyond? He'd lost all sense of direction.

"Hold up." He laboriously maneuvered his snowshoes to face Rachel. "Do you have any idea where we are?"

"Let me check my GPS. Oh, wait, I don't have a GPS. Or a map. Or a satellite photo."

He preferred her snarky attitude to fear. It was better for her not to know how much danger they might be in. "I want to get a general idea. When I picked you up, what was the closest town?"

"We were near Shadow Mountain Lake. There are a couple of resorts there but nothing resembling a town until Grand Lake."

"In terms of miles, how far?"

With her glove, she brushed a dusting of snow off her shoulder. "Hard to say. As the crow flies, only about five miles or so. But none of these roads are straight lines."

They could be winding back and forth for hours and making very little progress. "I hate mountains."

"A typical comment from a Southern California boy."

"Yeah? What have you got against palm trees and beaches?"

"Real men live in the mountains."

Though tempted to yank her into his arms and show her that he was a real man, he took his cell phone out of his pocket. Miracle of miracles, he had a signal!

"What is it?" Rachel asked.

"The phone works. Finally." He peeled off his glove, accessed his directory and called Agent Ted Waxman in

Los Angeles. California was an hour earlier and it was before seven o'clock here, but his primary FBI handler was available to him 24/7.

Waxman's mumbled hello made Cole think the agent was still in bed, warm and cozy under the covers.

"It's Cole. I need to come in from the cold. Literally."

"Where are you?" Waxman's voice had gone from drowsy to alert. "Do you have your GPS locator turned on?"

He wanted to believe he could trust Waxman. They weren't buddies; undercover agents didn't spend much face time inside the bureau offices. But Waxman had been his primary contact for almost four years.

Cole's phone didn't have much juice; he didn't waste words. "Give me an update. Fast."

"Turn on the GPS and go to a road," Waxman instructed. "We'll find you."

His suspicions about Agent Wayne Prescott and his possible involvement with the shooters from last night warned against giving away their location. "Who's looking for us?"

"Every law enforcement official in the state of Colorado, especially the FBI."

"Why? Give me the 4-1-1. What's going on?"

His pause spoke volumes. Waxman was a by-the-book agent who followed orders and trusted the system. If he'd been given instructions to withhold info, it would go against his nature to disobey. At the same time, he was Cole's handler, and it was his duty to protect his agent.

"Turn yourself in," Waxman said, "and we'll get this straightened out."

Turn myself in? That sounded like he was wanted for committing a crime. "The last time I contacted anybody was after the casino robbery. Prescott told me to stick with the gang. What's changed since then?"

Another pause. "Activate the damn GPS, Cole."

While he was at it, maybe he ought to paint a bull's-eye on his back. "Give me a reason."

"Don't play dumb with me. Three people are dead. And you're on the run with two of the gang members. You're considered to be armed and dangerous."

That description justified the use of lethal force in making an arrest. Cole saw their chances of a peaceful surrender disappearing. "Two other gang members?"

"One male and one female."

Somehow Rachel had been labeled as part of the gang. "You've got that wrong. The woman with me is—"

"Damn it, Cole. You kidnapped a baby."

The worst kind of crime. Violence against children. Cole was in even more trouble than he'd imagined. "Here's the true story. I'm close to identifying Baron, and he's running this show. Don't ask me how, but he's got people inside the Denver FBI office."

"A newborn infant." Waxman's voice rasped with anger. "You're using a baby as a hostage."

There would be no reasoning with him. Cole ended the call and turned off the phone, making sure the GPS wasn't on.

Rachel stared at him. Her eyes filled with questions. He didn't have the answers she'd want to hear.

RACHEL LISTENED WITH RISING DREAD as Cole recounted his conversation with Agent Waxman. They were the subjects of a manhunt? Considered to be dangerous? The FBI thought they had kidnapped Goldie?

"No," she said firmly. "People around here know me.

They'd know those accusations are wrong. As soon as they heard my name—"

"It's not likely that they've identified you."

"If they show my picture—"

"They won't."

In normal circumstances, she'd be missed at work. But this was her vacation; nobody would be looking for her. "The van," she said. "When I don't return the van to the clinic, the women I work with will know that something's wrong. I can contact them and get this all cleared up."

"Not a good idea."

"Why not?"

His face was drawn. His eyes were serious. "You saw what those men did last night at the house. It's best if we don't get anyone else involved."

"Are you saying that they'd go after my friends? My coworkers?"

"Not if they don't know anything."

She'd been cut off from anything resembling her normal life. The only person she could turn to was Cole, and she barely trusted him. "What's going to happen to Goldie?"

"We need to get her to a safe place. If we can find a cabin with reliable people, we'll leave her in their care."

She peered through the trees at the surrounding hillsides, which were buried in drifts and veiled in light snowfall. "We can turn ourselves in at the same time."

"It's not safe for us to be in custody. Not until we know who's working with Baron."

Inside her parka, she felt Goldie shift positions. The most important thing was to get the baby to safety. "Grand Lake. We need to go to Grand Lake. Penny told me that her mother was staying there. We'll take Goldie to her grandmother."

Cole reached out with his gloved hand and patted her shoulder. "You're a brave woman, Rachel. I'm sorry I got you into this mess."

"As long as you get me out of it, I'll be fine." She nodded toward the path ahead of them. "Make tracks."

She followed him, tramping through the snow on the path through the forest. The crampons on the snowshoes gave her stability, but the hike was exhausting. Though she couldn't see the incline, she knew they were headed uphill because of the strain on her thighs. Still, she was glad for the physical exertion. If she slowed down, she'd have to face her fear.

As an EMT, she'd worked with cops. She knew what "armed and dangerous" meant. She and Cole wouldn't have a chance to explain or defend themselves. The people looking for them would shoot first and ask questions later.

They approached a crossroads with open terrain on each side. The road was barely discernable under the mounds of snow, but a wooden street sign marked the corner.

Cole halted and squinted at the sign. "The road we're on is Lodgepole. The other is Lake Vista. Ring any bells?"

"Please don't ask me for directions." Grand County was huge, nearly two thousand square miles. Her condo was in Granby, which was forty-five minutes away from here. "I don't know this territory. I've only been to Grand Lake five or six times."

He looked over his shoulder at her. "It makes sense that the Lake Vista road will lead to water. We'd be more likely to find cabins at lakeside."

"But the other road goes uphill," she pointed out. "It offers a better vantage point."

She tilted back her head, looked up and glimpsed a hint of blue through the pale gray clouds. Good news: the snowfall was ending. Bad news: they were more exposed to the people who were searching for them.

"Do you hear that?" Cole asked.

"What?"

He sidestepped deeper into the forest. "Get back here."

Though she didn't hear anything, she did as he said, remembering how he'd sensed the attack at the house before the shooting started. She shuffled forward, taking cover behind the trunk of the same tree he stood behind.

Cole shifted his feet in the snowshoes so he was facing her. Quickly, he shed the huge backpack from his shoulders and moved closer to her.

She heard the sound of a vehicle. *They were coming.*

A black SUV crested the hill above the crossroads and ploughed a trail through the snow that covered the road. There were no markings on the vehicle; it wasn't a police car. She held her breath, waiting for them to pass.

The SUV drove past them, headed toward the cabin.

Cole took his cell phone from his pocket. Quickly, he dialed.

She heard his end of the conversation. "Waxman, this is Cole. There's a wounded man in a cabin on Lodgepole Road. He's tied down, helpless. The cabin isn't far from the house where we stayed last night."

He ended the call and put away his phone.

If the men in the SUV were the same shooters who attacked last night, Frank didn't stand a chance. Last night, she'd patched him up. Today, he could be murdered.

When she looked up at Cole, she felt a tear slip from the corner of her eye. "I wish things were different."

"There's nothing we can do for Frank." With his ungloved hand, he stroked her cheek and wiped away the tear. "They're close, Rachel. They'll be able to follow our tracks through the woods. We need to move fast."

There was no time for regret or recrimination. All her energy focused on pushing forward. They stayed in the trees, avoiding the road, but the forest was beginning to thin. Many of these trees had been lost to the pine beetle epidemic. The bare branches looked like gnarled fingers clawing at the snowy mist.

Rounding a boulder, Cole stopped so suddenly that she almost ran into him. She peered around his shoulder and saw the frozen expanse of Shadow Mountain Lake. Untouched, white and spectacularly beautiful, it was covered with snow, and the drifts swirled like vanilla frosting on a cake. Heavy clouds prevented her from seeing all the way to the opposite side.

"How wide is the lake?" Cole asked.

"It varies."

"How far from the town?"

"At the north end, it's only about a mile and a half farther to Grand Lake."

"If we cross it, we've got no cover," he said. "But we're running out of path. As soon as they pick up our trail, they'll know we're following the road."

She assumed the lake was frozen solid, but she didn't know for sure. If they broke through the ice, it would be over for them. And for Goldie. She imagined the dark, frigid waters beneath the pristine surface—waters that could suck them down to a terrible death.

Cole made a turn-around on his snowshoes and looked down at her. His eyes were warm. "We can do this."

"Or we could keep looking for a cabin." Hiking through a blizzard was one thing. Walking on a frozen lake—even when it appeared to be solid—was a risk. "I'm not sure this is safe."

"It's our best chance, Rachel."

He was right. She swallowed hard and nodded. "You go first."

They climbed down the incline leading to the frozen lake. As Cole stepped onto the surface, his snowshoes sank three or four inches into the snow. She clenched her jaw and listened for the cracking sound of ice breaking.

He strode ten feet onto the lake, breaking a path for her to follow. He turned back toward her and held out his gloved hand. "It's all going to be all right."

"How do you know?"

"I'm taking a leap of faith."

Cautiously, she stepped onto the lake. The snow sank beneath her snowshoes, and she caught her breath. Was it solid? Would it hold?

Cole caught hold of her gloved hand and squeezed. "Stay close."

"Do I have a choice?"

Lowering her head, she concentrated on putting her shoes in his tracks. One foot after the other, she followed. With every step, she prayed that the ice would hold.

For what seemed like an eternity, they made their way forward. Without the shelter of the forest, the fierce wind bit the exposed skin on her face. Inside her parka, she was warm. Goldie was protected by her body heat.

"I can see the other side," Cole said.

Looking back over her shoulder, she saw the long trail they'd left in the snow. The point where they'd started was barely visible through the snowy mist.

She saw something else.

A volley of gunfire exploded behind them.

Chapter Ten

The shooters had found them. The bursts from their semiautomatics boomed across the frozen landscape. Cole estimated they were over four hundred yards away on the other side of the lake—out of range unless they had a sniper rifle with a high-tech scope. Even with a more accurate weapon, their visibility would be hampered by the icy mist.

As he watched, the SUV lurched off the road. They were driving onto the lake.

He drew his handgun, ready to make a stand even though he was outmatched in terms of men and firepower. "Rachel, keep going."

"I can't leave you here."

"You need to get Goldie away from here."

Her internal struggle showed in her eyes. She didn't want to desert him, but the SUV was coming closer. The baby's safety came first.

"Don't die," she said. "I wouldn't be able to stand it if you—"

"Just go."

In her snowshoes, she rushed forward. The shoreline was so damned close. She had to make it into the forest. The bare limbs of trees reached toward her with the promise of shelter.

He looked back toward the SUV. They were coming

closer, but their forward progress was slow. The heavy vehicle sank down into the new snow. The drifts piled up higher than the hubcaps.

One of the gunmen leaned out a window and fired off another round—a sloppy tactic typical of a drive-by shooter who figured if he sprayed enough bullets he'd eventually hit something. These guys weren't trained to attack in open terrain, and they sure as hell weren't FBI.

These were Baron's men. Lethal. Bent on murder.

Cole shrugged off his huge backpack and dropped it onto the snow in front of him. The canvas pack and lightweight aluminum frame wasn't enough to stop a bullet, but it was something. Not taking off his snowshoes, he ducked behind the pack and waited. When they got closer, he'd aim for the windshield on the driver's side. If he could take out the man behind the wheel, he might slow them down long enough to make his escape.

The engine of the SUV whined as the tires failed to gain traction on the ice. Snow had accumulated in front of the SUV. The driver had to back up in his own tracks and push forward again.

From the trees, Rachel called to him. "I made it."

"Go deeper into the forest."

"Not without you."

The SUV jerked forward and back. The wheels were stuck. Two men emerged from the vehicle and staggered through knee-deep snow to the front bumper, where they started digging.

The weight of the SUV had to be close to two tons. Heavy enough to break through the ice? That was too much good luck to hope for.

For now, he should take advantage of the situation. They were distracted by being stuck. He might have enough time to make his escape before they started shooting again.

He slung the pack onto his shoulders, grabbed his ski poles and rushed along the trail Rachel had made through the snow. He reached the forest. Gunfire erupted. Cole dodged behind a boulder, where she stood waiting.

Breathing hard, he rested his back against the hard granite surface.

"We're good," Rachel said. "Even if they get themselves dug out, there's no access to a road on this side."

The muscles of his face tightened as he grinned. They just might make it to safety. "We got lucky."

"It's more than that."

"Yeah, those guys are idiots."

"And we were prepared," she said. "After all your complaining, I'll bet you're glad you have those snowshoes."

"Hell, yes. I'm thinking of having them permanently attached to my feet."

"You might be a real mountain man, after all."

Another wild blast of gunfire reminded him that they needed to keep moving. Even idiots were dangerous when well-armed. He shoved away from the rock. "When we get to the town, do you know how to find Penny's mother?"

"I do, indeed."

Until now, Rachel had been hesitant about giving directions. "What makes you so certain?"

"Penny called her mom after the baby was born and got the address, which she repeated several times."

"Why didn't she know her own mother's address?"

"Her mom doesn't actually live in Grand Lake. She's house-sitting for a friend who has a business in town. The house is around the corner from her friend's shop on the main street."

They'd be marching through the center of town. With every law enforcement officer in the state of Colorado looking for them, this might be tricky. "What kind of shop?"

"One that's closed in the winter," she said. "An ice cream parlor."

THEIR TREK INTO GRAND LAKE went faster than Rachel expected. It was still early, and the locals were just beginning to deal with the aftermath of last night's blizzard. A few were out with shovels. Others cleared their driveways and sidewalks with snowblowers. None of them paid much attention as she and Cole hiked along the road in their snowshoes.

The main tourist area was a rustic, Old West boardwalk with storefronts on either side. She spotted Lily Belle's Soda Fountain and Ice Cream Shop with a neatly lettered sign in the window: Closed for the Season.

In minutes they'd be at the house where Penny's mom was staying. Rachel was glad to be dropping Goldie off with someone who would care for her, but she wasn't looking forward to telling Penny's mom what had happened.

A young man with a snowblower finished clearing the sidewalk leading up to a two-story, cedar frame house. He turned toward them and waved. She waved back and yelled over the noisy machine. "Does Pearl Richards live here?"

He nodded and continued along the sidewalk to dig out the next house on the street.

Cole gave her a glance. "Penny's mother is named Pearl?"

"Pearl, Penny and Goldie," she said. "I guess they're all material girls."

Standing on the porch, they took off their snowshoes and knocked. A woman with curly blond hair pulled back in a ponytail opened the door a crack and peeked out. "Do I know you?"

"Penny gave me your address," Rachel said.

She pulled the door open, revealing a brightly colored patchwork jacket over jeans and a turtleneck. Though it was early, Pearl was fully dressed and wearing hiking boots as though she was prepared for action.

Pearl stepped back into the dim recesses of an old-fashioned looking parlor with drawn velvet curtains, an Oriental rug and an uncomfortable looking Victorian sofa with matching chaise. Pearl went to a claw-footed coffee table and picked up her revolver. Like Penny, she was a small, slight woman who needed both hands to aim her weapon.

Rachel should have been alarmed, but this greeting was so similar to the way she'd met Penny that she almost laughed out loud. Apparently, the women in this family routinely said hello with a gun.

"Close the door," Pearl said. "Young man, take off that backpack and that ridiculous leather jacket. You're dripping all over the floor."

As Cole removed his jacket, he said, "I'm armed."

"I expected as much." Pearl leveled her gun at the center of his chest. "Using your thumb and forefinger, place your weapon on the floor and step away from it."

Though Rachel suspected that this wasn't the first time Pearl had confronted an armed man, she still wasn't afraid. Either she was growing accustomed to having her life threatened or she sensed a basic goodness in this curly-haired woman who didn't look like she was much older than thirty.

"Both of you," Pearl said, "come through here to the kitchen. No sudden moves."

Rachel did as she was told. The huge kitchen, painted

a sunny yellow, had professional quality appliances and gleaming marble countertops. In no way did it resemble the antique parlor.

"The gun isn't necessary," Rachel said.

"I'll make that decision, missy. My daughter got herself tangled up with some bad folks. I'm not taking any chances."

"I'm a midwife," Rachel said. "I helped Penny deliver her baby."

Pearl's big brown eyes softened. "Goldie."

"She's right here." Rachel unzipped her parka and took it off to reveal the sling holding the infant. "And she's hungry."

"My granddaughter." Pearl's gun hand faltered. "But where's… Oh, no. Penny's dead, isn't she?"

"I'm sorry," Cole said.

He stepped forward, smoothly took the gun from Pearl and helped her into a chair at the kitchen table where she sat, stiff as a rail. Her unseeing eyes stared at the empty space opposite her.

"I knew this day would come." Pearl's voice dropped to a whisper. "Penny was always wild. Careless. I encouraged her to be a free spirit and to express herself, but she should have had more controls, more rules."

"I'll get you a glass of water," Cole said.

"Make it orange juice."

"Orange juice it is."

"With a shot of vodka. The booze is in the cabinet over the sink."

While he went to do Pearl's bidding, Rachel lifted Goldie out of the sling and set her down on the countertop to take off the purple snowsuit. The baby waved her arms, kicked and cooed. She was full of life, deserving of a chance at happiness.

Rachel hoped Pearl would be able to care for her granddaughter. “Penny said you were house-sitting. Where do you live?”

“I have a studio in Denver.”

“You’re an artist?”

“I do some painting. And I design jewelry. For a while, I had a shop in Grand Lake. When Penny was in her teens, I moved up here. I wanted to get her away from bad influences in the city.” She paused. “That didn’t work too well.”

“I only knew Penny for a short time,” Rachel said. “No matter how many unfortunate decisions she might have made in her life, she did the right things during her pregnancy. She wanted to give birth without drugs, wanted the best for her baby.”

“I had natural childbirth, too. I was only eighteen.” A thin smile played on Pearl’s full lips. “I wasn’t ready to settle down, drifted from place to place, fell into and out of love. But I always did right by my daughter. She was more precious to me than breath. That’s not to say we didn’t fight. The last time I saw her, I was so angry.”

“Did you know what she was doing?”

“I knew it wasn’t good. The fellow with her was a thug. I believe his name was Frank. He’s not the father, is he?”

“No,” Rachel said quickly.

“Thank God.” Pearl slowly shook her head. “I went looking for my daughter. Found her at a casino in Black Hawk. She stood there in the middle of all those slot machines with her belly bulging. I wanted to take her home with me, but she refused. I had hoped that when she was a mother, she’d understand.”

“I believe she did. When she saw Goldie for the first time, she glowed from inside. It was as though she’d swallowed a candle.”

Cole placed the vodka and orange juice on the table. "Penny couldn't stop smiling. She was beautiful."

Pearl lifted the glass to her lips and took a sip. Thus far, she had avoided looking at her grandchild. Glass in hand, she stood and snapped at Cole. "Come with me into the other room. I want to know what happened to Penny. Tell me everything."

They left the kitchen, but Cole returned almost immediately with the backpack. "You need to get Goldie changed and fed. I don't think we can leave her here."

"Penny wanted her mother to take the baby."

"I'm not sure Pearl can handle an infant."

An aura of sorrow veiled his features, and she knew that he was feeling guilt for Penny's death. Rachel understood. Logically, he'd know that her murder wasn't his fault. He hadn't pulled the trigger. He hadn't put Penny in danger. But he'd take responsibility the same way she'd blamed herself when she lost a patient.

He stood and straightened. When he walked back to the parlor, he looked stoic as though preparing to face a firing squad. His conversation with Pearl was going to be difficult, but it had to be done.

She looked down at Goldie and smoothed the fringe of downy brown hair that framed her round face. "What are we going to do with you?"

The baby gurgled in response. Her shining eyes fixed on the light from the window above the yellow café curtains.

Dragging this darling infant all over the frozen countryside simply wasn't an option. They'd been lucky so far; Goldie had stayed safe and warm, snuggled against her chest. But so many things could have gone wrong. If Penny's mother couldn't take the baby, they'd have to risk going to the police and handing Goldie to them.

As Rachel went through the procedures of preparing formula, she tried to imagine what would happen if they turned themselves in. Cole was in far more danger than she was. As soon as her identity was verified, she ought to be all right. After all, she had an alibi for the time when the gang was on the run. She'd been delivering a baby. *Jim Loughlin's baby.*

She caught her breath. Oh, God, why hadn't she thought of this before? Big Jim Loughlin was a deputy. She could call on him to help her.

The yellow phone hanging on the wall by the kitchen cabinets beckoned to her. Though she didn't know the Loughlins' phone number off the top of her head, information would have it. But if she used this phone, it would pinpoint her location. Other people could track them down to this house.

Deputy Loughlin was the answer to all their problems. She couldn't wait to tell Cole.

When he returned to the kitchen with Pearl, Rachel was glad to see that the vodka and orange juice had barely been touched. The older woman came directly to her. "I'm ready to meet Goldie."

Rachel placed the baby in her grandmother's arms. The bonding was instantaneous. The pained tension on Pearl's face transformed into adoring tenderness, and she exhaled in a sweet, soft hum.

Rachel exhaled a sigh of relief. Goldie was going to be just fine with her grandma.

Chapter Eleven

While Pearl settled down on the parlor sofa to feed Goldie her bottle, Rachel took Cole into the kitchen. She kept her voice low, not wanting to disturb the moment of bonding between grandma and baby. But she felt like singing. Their problems were all but over.

She beamed at Cole. In his black turtleneck and still-damp jeans, he looked big, rough and intimidating, until he smiled back and she saw the warmth in his eyes. He came closer. With his thumb, he tilted her chin up, and she thought he was going to kiss her again.

His voice was a whisper. "What's going on? You look like you just found the pot of gold at the end of the rainbow."

"Jim Loughlin," she said. "Deputy Jim Loughlin. He'll help us."

"Why do you think so?"

"Don't you see?" Excitement bubbled through her. "This is the perfect solution."

He rested his palm on her forehead. "That's funny. You don't feel feverish."

"I'm not delusional." She took a step back. "Once I contact Jim, we'll be in the clear. In fact, the police will probably thank us."

"Before you schedule our ticker tape parade, take a breath. Sit down."

"Why are you being so negative?"

"Start at the beginning. Who's Loughlin?"

She plunked into a chair at the kitchen table. "The house I was at before you kidnapped me belongs to Jim and Sarah Loughlin. Jim happens to be a deputy sheriff. If I call him, he can arrange for us to turn ourselves in."

"You believe that you trust him."

"One hundred and ten percent," she said confidently. "Jim would do anything for me. I just went through the labor-and-birthing process with him and his wife. They think I'm pretty terrific."

"Which you are."

"Thank you."

He wasn't responding with the enthusiasm she'd expected. As he took a seat beside her, his forehead furrowed. His cognac-brown irises turned a deeper, darker shade. "Let's think about it before you call him."

"What's to think about? We turn ourselves in, and he calls off the manhunt."

"After which," Cole said, "your friend will be ordered to turn us over to Wayne Prescott and the FBI."

"Not necessarily."

"It's his job. Even if Loughlin thinks you walk on water, he can't go against orders. Prescott is calling the shots."

She hadn't thought that far ahead. "But the Loughlins know I'm innocent. They're my alibi. I was with them when you were on the run. They know I'm not a criminal."

"Neither am I." Gently, he took her hand. "But Prescott has somehow managed to turn my FBI handler against me."

"I still want to call Jim," she said. "Your cell phone doesn't have GPS tracking, right?"

He took it out of his pocket and placed the phone on the table. “Give it a shot. Put the call on speaker so I can hear.”

She’d already used Pearl’s phone to call information and get the home number for the Loughlins. She punched it into Cole’s cell. *This plan will work. It has to work.*

As soon as Jim answered, she said, “This is Rachel. How’s the baby doing? Do you have a name yet?”

“Caitlyn,” he said. “She’s beautiful.”

“And Sarah?”

“I didn’t think it was possible to love my wife more than the day we were married, but I’m in awe of this woman—the mother of my child.”

He was the kind of guy who renewed her faith in the goodness of humanity. She felt guilty about intruding on his happiness with her problems. “What have you heard about the casino robbers?”

“There’s a big-deal manhunt. Everybody on duty is looking for the three that got away. They’ve got roadblocks set up. They were trying to monitor the on-the-road cameras, but a lot of them got messed up by the snow. Why do you ask?”

“The woman fugitive,” she said. “The supposed woman fugitive is me.”

There was a silence. He cleared his throat and his deep voice dropped all the way into the cellar. “What are you talking about?”

“After I left your house, I was kidnapped by the robbers to help a woman in the gang deliver her baby. You must have suspected something. My van was at the house where the three people were killed.”

“I haven’t heard anything about your van. As far as I know the three victims were found by the FBI in a clearing right before the blizzard hit.”

"Not in a house?"

"No."

A cover-up. She should have expected as much. Penny had told her that the house belonged to Baron; he wouldn't want to be associated with them.

Quietly, Cole said, "Tell him you have an address."

She spoke up, "I can give you the location of—"

"Is somebody with you?" Jim asked.

"Yes." She wouldn't lie. "I'm with a man who was part of the gang, but he's really an undercover FBI agent. A good guy. He saved my life. And the baby's."

"You have the baby with you," Jim said.

"If we'd left her behind, they would have killed her. You have to believe me."

"Where are you, Rachel?"

She looked at Cole, who shook his head. Sadly, she agreed with him. If she told Jim where she was, the police would be at the door, and they'd be handed over to the people who wanted them dead.

"I can't tell you. There's a conspiracy going on that's too complicated to explain. If I'm taken into FBI custody, I'll be arrested or made to disappear. Or killed."

"Is that what this undercover fed told you? Rachel, you have to get away from him. He's no good."

"Deputy Loughlin," Cole said with calm authority, "you know Rachel isn't a criminal. She's a healer. To protect her, it's imperative that you tell no one about this phone call."

"Don't tell me about protecting Rachel." Jim's voice rumbled. "I'd do anything for her."

"I'm counting on your silence," Cole said. "I'm going to give you an address. It's the house where the murders took place. Even if the blood has been cleaned up, there will be evidence of a shoot-out. Check the property records and find the name of the owner. Tell no one what you're doing."

"I won't help you. That's aiding and abetting."

"Please," Rachel said. "I need your help, Jim."

Cole gave him the address. "We'll call you back."

As he disconnected the call and slipped the phone into his pocket, Rachel felt her high hopes come crashing to the ground. She couldn't trust anyone. Not even Jim.

COLE PULLED OPEN the heavy velvet drapes in the front parlor and looked outside. Above the snow-laden rooftops, he saw the clouds breaking up and the sky turning blue. Sunlight glistened on mounds of snow piled beside the sidewalks. Kids in parkas and snow hats were having a snowball fight. People waved to each other. A four-wheel-drive vehicle bounced along the plowed street in front of the house.

His undercover work generally led him into rat-infested back alleys and strip joints. Not here. Not to small town America, where you couldn't see the criminals until they held a knife to your throat.

He turned away from the window.

The scene inside the house was equally charming. Rachel and Pearl sat beside each other on the fancy Victorian sofa. Their heads bent down; the curly blond bangs on Pearl's forehead almost touched Rachel's sleek dark hair as they fussed over the baby.

There wasn't time for cooing infants and cozy musing after the storm. He and Rachel had managed to find Penny's mother without too much difficulty. Sooner or later, Baron's men would do the same. They could be surrounding the place at this very moment.

"Ladies," he snapped.

Pearl looked up at him. Though her lips smiled, her

expression was flat. Something inside her had died. When he'd talked to her earlier, she had demanded the truth about her daughter's death. He'd tried to be gentle, but as he spoke, he'd seen the cold embrace of despair and sorrow squeeze the light from her eyes.

Beside her, Rachel had slipped into an attitude of outward calm that masked her internal tension. She'd looked the same way when she directed Penny through the last stage of labor.

These two women weren't kidding themselves. No matter how unflustered they looked, both were aware of the tragedy and the danger. They needed him to point the way.

"Here's what we're going to do," he said. "First we get Pearl and Goldie to safety."

"Agreed," Pearl said. "I can't stay here. Too many people in town know that I'm house-sitting."

"Deputy Loughlin said there were roadblocks and surveillance cams, but they won't be looking for you. Take Goldie and get onto the highway as soon as possible."

"You need a car seat," Rachel said.

"Not a problem. The woman who owns this house has a couple of car seats in the closet of the guest bedroom for when her grandchildren come to visit in the summer." She looked down at the sleeping baby on her lap. "Don't worry, little one. Grammy Pearl is going to take good care of you."

"You shouldn't return to your home in Denver," he said. "Not until we know it's safe."

When she nodded, her curly blond ponytail bounced. "Maybe I can stay with a friend in Granby. She was Penny's favorite teacher in high school. Taught economics and history."

"Does she still teach there?" Rachel asked. "I might know her. I do health programs at the high school."

"Jenna Cambridge."

"A teacher?" Rachel lifted an eyebrow. "Penny talked about Jenna as though she was more of a friend."

"That boundary might have gotten a bit fuzzy. Jenna was new in town and lonely. Plain as dishwater. She liked to go out with Penny." Her lip trembled. "My daughter attracted attention wherever she went."

Though Cole had known Penny for less than a month, he had to agree. Even nine months pregnant, Penny was a firecracker. "Did Jenna know Penny's boyfriends?"

"More than I did." Pearl swiped a tear from the corner of her eye. "Penny didn't tell me much about the guys she dated."

Gently, Rachel said, "One of them might be Goldie's father. Penny said they started dating when she was in high school. He was an older man."

"How much older?"

"He took her to a classy places, bought her expensive gifts." Rachel circled her wrist with her fingers. "A diamond tennis bracelet."

"Those were real?"

"According to Penny."

"How could I miss that? I'm a jewelry designer." Pearl's features hardened. Anger was beginning to replace her sadness. "Not that I work with precious gems. Amethyst is about as fancy as I get. And pearls, of course."

He noticed that she was wearing silver teardrop earrings and a ring with three black pearls. Her only bit of artistic flamboyance was her colorful patchwork jacket. He liked her flair and her earthy sensibility.

Rachel cleared her throat. "Does the name Wayne Prescott mean anything to you?"

She frowned as she considered. Her hand absently patted Goldie's backside. "I don't know him. Is he the father?"

"I don't know."

"Tell me more about this older man."

"Penny didn't actually say how they met, but I got the idea that he was somehow connected to her school. Not a teacher, though. Maybe the father of another student. She said that Jenna told her he was Penny's Mister Big—the man she'd spend the rest of her life with."

"Jenna knew? All of a sudden, I don't want to see her or talk to her. Why wouldn't she tell me?"

"Penny probably asked her not to."

"I never guessed that Penny was dating an adult man. She was only seventeen when she waltzed through the door with that bracelet." She shot a hard glance at Cole. "If she was sleeping with him, that's rape, isn't it?"

He nodded. "This older man is the mastermind behind the gang and the robberies. They call him Baron."

Still holding Goldie, she surged to her feet. "And he's the father."

"Yes."

"I want you to catch this bastard."

Cole had come to the same conclusion. He and Rachel couldn't run forever. The only way they'd be able to turn themselves in to the cops would be if they had solid, irrefutable evidence against Baron. They needed to go on the offensive.

"We can start by talking to Jenna," he said. "She might know Baron's real name."

"I'll make the call," Pearl said as she handed the sleeping baby to Rachel.

In the kitchen, Cole went over a few things Pearl needed to avoid mentioning. Obviously, she couldn't tell Jenna about him or Rachel. And it was best not to mention that she had Goldie with her. Penny's high school teacher had already kept one secret from Pearl. "She's not entirely trustworthy."

"You can say that again." Pearl gave a brisk nod. "Listen, Cole. I'm a pretty good actress. Just tell me what to say."

"You want to get the father's name. That's number one."

"Got it."

"Pretend that you never saw us. Say that you had a call from Penny and she had her baby." He glanced at the clock on the stove. "It's after nine. Will Jenna be at work?"

"Not today. The kids are out of school because of the blizzard."

He handed Pearl his cell phone, which had been recharging for the past hour. "Make the call. Put it on speaker."

Jenna answered on the third ring. Her greeting was overly effusive—as giggly as the teenagers she taught. "I haven't seen you in ages, Pearl. How are you?"

"I'm worried," she said. "Penny called last night and said she had her baby, but I haven't been able to get in touch with her. Did she call you?"

"Boy or girl?"

"Girl. Her name is Goldie," Pearl said.

"Congratulations, grandma. You must be so happy."

"Must be." Sadness tugged at the corners of Pearl's lips, but she kept her voice upbeat. "I sure wish I knew the baby's daddy. I think it was somebody she dated in high school. Did she mention him to you?"

"Penny has so many boyfriends. I can't keep track."

"This one was special. He gave her that sparkly tennis bracelet."

"Sorry. I don't remember."

Cole didn't believe Jenna. Penny would have been sure

to brag about her diamonds, and she'd told Rachel that Jenna was her confidante.

Pearl said, "She called him Mister Big."

"Like *Sex and the City.*" She giggled. "I guess Penny is the Granby version of high fashion."

"Are you sure," Pearl said, "that you don't remember him?"

"Not at all, but I'll let you know when Penny contacts me. I'm sure she'll turn up. Like a bad penny."

"Why?" Pearl's voice betrayed her rising frustration. "Why are you so sure she'll contact you?"

"For one thing, we're friends. For another, she's been sending me these mysterious packages to hold for her."

Jenna was the contact.

Penny had been using her high school teacher as the drop-off person after the robberies. She'd been sending Jenna bundles of loot.

Chapter Twelve

As hideouts went, the office in the back of Lily Belle's Soda Fountain and Ice Cream Shop was okay. At least, Rachel thought so. She would have preferred staying in the house, but too many people knew Pearl was living there. Lily Belle's was empty, closed for the season, and it had an alarm system.

She and Cole would stay here until nightfall. According to his FBI training, the first twenty-four hours were considered to be the most crucial in a manhunt. After that, the intensity would let up, and they'd make their move.

Rachel slipped off her parka and lowered herself onto the mint-green futon. After sending Pearl on her way with Goldie and the massive backpack filled with baby supplies, she felt unencumbered and a hundred times less tense. All she had to worry about was her own safety and Cole's.

After closing the office door and placing their food supplies on the coffee table in front of the futon, he prowled around the windowless, peach-colored room. The top of the cream-painted desk was empty except for a day-by-day calendar, a pencil jar that looked like an ice cream cone and a couple of framed photographs of smiling, blue-eyed kids. Lily's grandchildren, no doubt. A row of three-drawer cabinets in pastel colors lined the back wall. Bouquets of fake flowers in matching pastel vases sat atop them. A light coat of dust covered every surface. Otherwise, the office was clean. The lingering scent of vanilla and buttery cream hung in the air.

"Too cutesy," he muttered.

"Like Willie Wonka. But with ice cream."

He checked the thermostat. "Good thing we brought blankets. It's set at fifty-two degrees."

"Sounds about right. Warm enough to keep things from freezing but not wasteful. Nobody is supposed to be here until the summer season."

He sank onto the futon beside her. "Take off your shoes."

"Why?"

"We should explore this place, and I don't want to leave wet footprints in case somebody looks through the front window."

With a groan, she wiggled her butt deeper into the futon cushion and stretched her legs out in front of her. Her thigh muscles ached after their crack-of-dawn trek across Shadow Mountain Lake in snowshoes. "What's the point of looking around? Nobody knows we're here. We're safe."

"Are we?"

"Please let me pretend—just for a moment—that crazy people with guns aren't trying to kill us."

"That's not your style," he said. "You're realistic. Practical. You don't delude yourself."

His snap analysis was pretty much on target, but she didn't want him to get cocky. "What makes you think you know me?"

"I'm a trained observer."

She supposed that was true. "In your undercover work, I guess you need to be able to figure out how people are going to act. To be thinking one step ahead."

"That's right."

"But that's on the surface. On a deeper level, you don't know me at all."

He dropped his boots onto the pink-and-green patterned area rug. "I've had a chance to observe your behavior in high-stress situations. I know how you'll react."

"But you don't know why," she said. "You can't tell what I'm thinking. You don't know what's going on inside my head."

He turned toward her and stared—stared hard as though he could actually see her brain working. The two days' growth of stubble on his chin and his messy hair made him look rough, rugged and sexy. Her gaze shifted from his eyes to his lips.

The corner of his mouth twitched into a grin. Then he came across the futon and leaned in close. The suddenness of his kiss took her breath away.

Without thinking, she wrapped her arms around his torso and pulled him against her. His mouth worked against hers. His tongue pushed through her lips.

In spite of her exhaustion, her body responded with a surge of excitement. She didn't feel the chill in the room, didn't look for an escape, didn't want to do anything but prolong this contact.

Ever since their kiss in the cabin, she'd been waiting for this moment—a time when they were finally alone. She had every intention of making love to Cole, but she didn't want to give in too fast. She wanted him to work for it.

Abruptly, she ended the kiss and pulled away from him. But only a few inches away. His face filled her field of vision, and she was captivated by the shimmer in his light brown eyes.

He murmured, "Is that what you were thinking?"

Was she that obvious? Did she radiate a vibe that told

him she was a single, thirty-something woman who needed a big, strong man? "You tell me."

"You kissed me back," he said.

"Just being polite."

"Here's what I know about you," he said. "You're smart, competent and pretty. You're at a good place in your life, and you love your work."

"I sound good," she said. "You're lucky to be in the same room with me."

"You're brave. But you're also scared."

Apparently, the compliment train had come to an end. The gleam in his eyes sharpened as he assessed her. He said, "You've been hurt."

"Who hasn't?"

As smoothly as he'd pounced on her, he adjusted his position so he was sitting beside her. "Who hurt you, Rachel? What happened?"

She thought of the men who had passed through her life, ranging from motorcycle man to a rocker with more tattoos than brains. That array of losers wasn't her greatest hurt.

"A six-year-old boy," she said.

She had never talked about this. *Never.* The memory was too painful, too devastating. Her memory of that boy sucked the air from her lungs.

"His name," she said, "was Adam."

He held her hand. "Go on."

"I'd rather not."

After this crisis was over, she didn't honestly expect to see him again. He would go back to California and be an undercover fed. She'd stay here and continue with her midwife career. They were like the proverbial ships passing in the night—if ships were capable of stopping at sea and having hot sex. Bottom line: she didn't need to reveal the dark corners of her soul to him.

He squeezed her hand. "Do you want to talk about what happened with Adam?"

"You're not going to give up on this, are you?"

"No pressure." He sat back on the futon and turned his gaze away from her. His profile was relaxed and calm. He was waiting; his message was clear.

If she wanted to talk, he'd listen. If not, she could keep her secrets buried. It certainly would be less complicated to grab him and proceed with the passion they were both feeling, but the words were building up inside her. If she didn't speak, she might explode.

"I'd been working as an EMT for a year and a half," she said. "I'd seen a lot. Traffic accidents. Heart attacks. Gunshot wounds. The work was getting to me. I was on the verge of a burnout."

She remembered the sunny summer day in Denver—the kind of day when you should be taking a puppy on a walk through a grassy green park. "We got the call and responded. It was a fire and an explosion in an apartment complex."

"Meth lab?"

"I don't know how it happened. Somebody probably told me, but the facts went out of my head."

The details blurred in her memory, but she felt a stab in her gut as she recalled the scene in a central courtyard with three-story buildings on all four sides. The smell of grit and smoke and blood came back to her.

"When we got there, rescuers were pulling people out of the buildings. Other ambulances had already arrived, and a senior EMT had taken charge. He assigned me to triage the wounded while my partner loaded the ambulance and took the more serious burn victims to the nearest hospital."

In minutes, her uniform had been covered in greasy soot and blood as she tended to the survivors. First-, second- and third-degree burns. Wounds caused by the shrapnel from the explosion. Someone had fallen down a flight of stairs.

"That's when I met Adam. A sweet-faced kid. He was lying on a sheet on the ground, and he didn't seem to be badly injured. His head was bleeding. The laceration didn't appear to be deep. When I started working on him, he looked up at me and smiled. He told me his name, and he promised he'd be all right. His exact words were…I'm not going to die."

A swell of emotion rose up inside her. She told herself that not everyone could be saved, but that truth did little to assuage the pain of her sorrow. She'd been hurt. God, yes, she'd been hurt. Not by a person but by life.

When Cole wrapped his arm around her and pulled her close, she didn't object. Her cheek rested against his chest; his solid presence comforted her.

In a whisper, she continued, "I left Adam. Went to deal with other victims. A woman with a broken leg called out Adam's name. His mother. Somehow, they'd gotten separated. She was frantic."

Rachel hadn't wasted time trying to calm Adam's mother. She'd gone back to the boy. His injuries had seemed less traumatic. She'd thought she could carry him and reunite the boy with his mother. "He was dead."

She'd tried to resuscitate the child. CPR. Straight oxygen. Mouth-to-mouth. Nothing worked. "I couldn't bring him back."

"Is that when you changed jobs?"

"Shortly after that." She shrugged. It wasn't necessary to talk about the months of debilitating depression and anger. The important thing was that she'd fought her way

There's room to hide behind the counter and the coolers. If worse comes to worst, you can bust through the windows. In the back, there's only one exit."

"Lovely." She smiled at him. "You know what makes me really sad?"

"What's that?"

"Looking at all this, I'm dying for some ice cream. Maybe a fudge sundae with whipped cream on top."

"Sounds like you need a little sweetness."

He slung his arm around her waist and yanked her toward him with such force that her feet came off the floor. He pressed her tightly against him and kissed her hard. There was nothing tentative about his approach; the idea of making love was a foregone conclusion. He was aggressive, fierce, demanding.

And she liked it.

Chapter Thirteen

The creamy pastel ambience in the office contrasted the hot red fire of their passion. Rachel felt like she ought to turn the desktop photographs of Lily Belle's grandchildren facedown so they wouldn't be traumatized. Her spirits rose and her excitement soared as Cole tore off her panties.

Breathing hard, she wrapped her arms around his neck and clung to him. Her right leg coiled around his, and she pressed herself against his erection.

His hand grabbed her butt and held her in place. He arched his neck and tilted his head back. For a moment, she thought he might start howling like a wolf. Then he lowered his head and consumed her with a kiss. His hands explored her body with rough caresses.

She felt herself turning into a quivering mass of jelly, unable to stand. They slid to the floor. On the pink-and-green patterned carpet, he straddled her and sat back, looking down.

His body amazed her. Muscular arms. Lean torso. Smooth chest. When she reached toward him, he cuffed her wrists in his grasp.

"No fair." She gasped. "I want to touch."

"How bad do you want it?"

She tried to pull her hands free, but he held her wrists firmly. He was in complete control. Or so he thought.

She widened her eyes and softened her voice. "Please, Cole. You're hurting me."

Concern flashed in his eyes. Immediately, he released his grasp.

And she took advantage. She rose up and twisted her body, throwing him off balance. Now she was on top. "Gotcha."

"You win."

He lay on his back with his arms sprawled above his head while she fondled, stroked and pinched. Her fingers glided along the ridges of his muscles. Leaning down, she nuzzled his chest and torso. Her excitement was building to a fever pitch. She didn't want to wait for one more second.

"Condom?" she asked.

"Wallet."

She crawled across the carpet to where he'd discarded his jeans. Was it really necessary to stop for a condom? Of course, it was. She gave lectures on the importance of protected sex. She had to do this.

After clumsy fumbling, she held the tiny see-through package in her hand. "It's blue."

"The only ones they had in super, gigantic, extra large."

He took charge again, and she let him. When he plunged into her, she gave a sharp cry. Her last coherent thought was that this was the best sex she'd ever had. Then she abandoned herself to the sheer physical pleasure of their lovemaking.

When it was over, she was shivering from head to toe. Not because it was fifty-two degrees in the room. This was a sensual release that had been building in her for years.

For the first time, she wondered if there might be a future for her and Cole.

COLE WANTED TO SPEND the rest of the day making love to Rachel. Their hideout in the office of the ice cream parlor seemed insulated from the rest of the world. After he converted the futon into a bed and spread out blankets, they were cozy and comfortable.

He lay on his back, and she snuggled her head against his shoulder. Cuddling had never been one of his favorite things, but he was betting that this cuddle would lead to something more.

"I only had the one rubber," he said.

"That could be a problem." She rose up on an elbow and looked down at him. "I'm guessing that Lily Belle doesn't keep a condom supply in her desk."

He looked up at her, memorizing every detail. Until now, she'd been so bundled up in turtlenecks and sweaters that he hadn't been able to appreciate her. From the neck down, she was firm but not too muscular and surprisingly graceful from the arch of her back to the crook of her elbow. Her throat was as smooth as ivory. He liked her short hair; it suited her face. Her high forehead balanced a strong, stubborn jaw. And her eyes? Those big blue eyes sparkled with humor and excitement.

He already wanted her again. "Would it help if I told you I recently had a physical, and I'm clean?"

"I give health lectures about bad boys like you. You wouldn't believe the stories high school boys come up with when they're trying to get their girlfriends to say yes."

"Actually, I'm familiar with those stories."

She traced a line down his nose and across his lips. "You and me? We're not in high school. Nothing you could say would convince me. It's my decision whether or not I take a risk."

They had bigger threats to worry about than unprotected

sex. Armed killers could burst through the door at any given moment. He needed to deal with that situation.

Reaching toward the coffee table, he picked up the cell phone and turned it on. "I want to check in with Pearl and see how she's doing."

"Put it on speaker," Rachel said.

Pearl answered right away on her hands-free phone. Her voice was chipper. "I got on the highway with no problem. The snowplows have been out, and I'm making good time."

"Any roadblocks?"

"None that I've seen. But there were a whole lot of police cars on the road when I was leaving Grand Lake."

"Are you headed to Jenna's house?"

"Certainly not. I'd rather camp in the forest than see that lying, little snake again. I'm staying with a friend in Denver. She has a penthouse condo in a secure building. We ought to be safe."

He was glad to hear that Pearl was taking the threat seriously.

Rachel piped up, "How's Goldie?"

"Sleeping in the car seat, snug as a bug. I might have to stop and give her a bottle, but I want to get out of the high country. There's more bad weather coming in."

"How bad?" he asked.

"Another eight to ten inches. On the radio, the ski areas are whooping and hollering about great conditions."

More snow presented an obstacle. He wanted to drive to Granby tonight, to talk with Jenna Cambridge and take possession of the packages Penny had sent to her. "Take care of yourself, Pearl. We'll call again later. Don't tell anyone else where you are."

"I understand."

"Give Goldie a hug," Rachel said.

He disconnected the call and looked toward her. She was sitting up on the futon, wide awake and alert, with a blanket around her shoulders to keep warm. He asked, "How are you at driving in snow?"

"Better than you, California boy."

"I'm good in a high-speed chase."

"What about black ice?"

"Have I mentioned how much I hate the mountains?"

"Seriously," she said, "the highway ought to be okay. The real problem will come when we get to Granby. Side roads don't get cleared too often. Since Pearl took the four-wheel drive SUV that belongs to Lily Belle, we're driving her little compact—not the best vehicle for deep snow."

"Do you think we can make it?"

"I don't know," she said. "If we run into trouble, we're caught."

It wouldn't be too bad to stay here overnight. He and Rachel could find plenty of ways to amuse themselves. "Let's call your cop buddy and see what he's found out."

Like Pearl, Deputy Jim Loughlin was quick to pick up. Had he been hovering by the phone, waiting for their call? Cole wanted to trust this guy because Rachel did, but he was realistic about the responsibilities of a law enforcement officer. At some point, Loughlin would have to obey orders. His tone was anxious. "Are you all right? Can you tell me if you're all right?"

"I'm good." She gave Cole a sultry smile. "Better than you'd expect."

"I went to the address you gave me," Loughlin said. "You were right. There was blood all over. Bullet holes. Looked like a semiautomatic weapon."

"Did you report it?" she asked.

"I should have, but I didn't." He grumbled, "I couldn't

figure out how to tell the sheriff without mentioning that I'd been in contact with you."

"Sorry to put you in this position," Cole said.

"Not your fault. There's something about this manhunt that just doesn't ring true. For starters, Rachel, you're obviously not a criminal."

"Thanks," she said. "What else bothers you?"

"The sheriff stopped by to see the baby. By the way, Sarah appreciates those instructions you left behind about breast feeding. My mom kept telling her that the bottle was better, but Sarah won't hear of it."

"Good for Sarah."

Cole told himself to be patient while the deep, rumbling voice of Deputy Loughlin talked about being a new daddy. His chat about breast feeding made a strange counterpoint to the massacre of the gang, but it was best to let Rachel's friend take his time.

"Anyway," Loughlin said, "there was an FBI agent with the sheriff. A guy by the name of Prescott."

Son of a bitch. Cole could think of only one reason why Prescott would be there. He knew about Rachel and wanted to get a lead on her whereabouts. It was looking more and more like Agent Wayne Prescott was a link to Baron.

Rachel asked, "What did Prescott want to know?"

"Here's the funny thing about him. He claimed that he doesn't know this area, but he used the names of local landmarks. Things like Pete's Pie Shack and Hangman's Tree. Stuff you wouldn't find on a map."

"You thought he was fishy?"

"Something about him didn't smell right," Loughlin said. "Then he asked me about you and the clinic. He mentioned your vacation and asked if we knew where you were going. But he never identified you as the female fugitive. The only name that's been given is Cole Bogart."

She shot him a questioning glance. Bogart wasn't the name he'd told her; that was his undercover identity.

Loughlin continued, "You're both described as being armed and dangerous based on the murders of those three people. But if you killed them, how did you remove the bodies? And why?"

"Somebody wants to keep the house where they were killed a secret," Cole said. "Did you check the records to find the owner?"

"It's a corporate group called Baron Enterprises. The primary name is Xavier Romero, who happens to be the owner of the Black Hawk casino that got robbed."

Cole knew that name, knew it well. Xavier Romero had been a small-time operator in the Southern California gambling scene. He was also a snitch—a likable old guy but shifty as a snake. Cole hadn't known that Romero owned the casino they hit.

Deputy Loughlin cleared his throat. "This just doesn't add up. Why would the gang hide in a house that belongs to the guy they robbed?"

Xavier Romero had to be in on the plot. Cole asked, "How much does Romero claim was stolen?"

"Over a hundred thousand."

Cole shook his head. "It wasn't half that much."

"The robbery report stated the higher amount," Jim said, "which means the insurance company will pay out the hundred thousand to the casino."

"Unless we can prove fraud," Cole said. "We need to find that money."

"We're talking about a lot of cash." The deputy's voice took on a note of suspicion. "I've never met you, Cole. I'm putting a lot of trust in you based on what Rachel says. Don't let me down."

"I won't," he promised.

"Thank you, Jim," Rachel said. "We'll be in touch as soon as we know anything else. Give Caitlyn a kiss from me."

She ended the call and turned to him. "Is that the answer you were looking for? Is Xavier Romero really the Baron?"

"Not possible. Romero is close to seventy. A potbellied old man with thinning white hair and thick glasses. His hands look arthritic, but he can make the cards dance when he's dealing poker."

"He must be Baron's associate. They're part of the same group that owns the house. And it sounds like he intends to commit insurance fraud with Baron's help."

"Right on both counts, partner."

She shook her head. "I'm not your partner in crime. Or crime solving. I'm not cut out for this undercover life."

"It's a gift," he said.

"Is it, Mister Bogart?"

"That's my undercover name. Cole Jeremy McClure is the name on my birth certificate."

"You didn't lie to me." She snuggled down beside him. Her flesh molded to his. "That makes me feel good."

He pulled her close. There were a number of things he ought to be thinking about: logistical problems in driving through another damn blizzard to Granby at night and the usefulness of calling Waxman with the new information about Xavier Romero. But his brain was clouded by her nearness. The scent of her body made him stupid. And happy.

He brushed his lips across her forehead and looked

into her eyes. "How do you feel about making love *sans* condom?"

"I'm for it," she said.

"What if you get pregnant?"

"This is something I never thought I'd hear myself say. Never. Do you understand? Never."

"I get it."

"But the truth is that I wouldn't mind getting pregnant. At this point in my life, I'm ready to have a baby."

His heart made a loud thud. His pulse stopped. He was lying naked with a woman who wanted a baby. *Danger, danger, danger.* "Excuse me?"

She laughed. "I've never seen the blood drain from someone's face so fast. Are you going into shock? Should I start CPR?"

"I'm cool."

"If I should happen to get pregnant, I wouldn't saddle you with any responsibilities. Being a single mom isn't my first choice. But I'm in my thirties, and I want kids. I love kids. And it's entirely possible that I'm not cut out for the whole marriage thing."

"Marriage?" He choked out the word. Was she trying to give him a heart attack?

"Don't worry, Cole. I'm not looking for a relationship with you. How could I? You live in California. And you have an incredibly dangerous job. Frankly, I wouldn't marry you on a bet."

His mood swung one hundred and eighty degrees. Because she said she'd never marry him, he had an urge to propose. "Are you giving me a preemptive rejection?"

"Absolutely. Long-distance relationships hardly ever work. And your undercover work scares me."

"Doesn't seem fair," he muttered.

"Don't feel bad. I consider you to be an excellent sperm

donor. You're intelligent, and you seem to be healthy. There aren't any weird genetic diseases lurking around in your DNA, are there?"

"Not that I know of."

She slipped her fingertips down his chest. "I don't think we need to worry about not having a condom."

When he kissed her, he was thinking of more than her slim, supple body. In his mind, he visualized a home with Rachel. She'd be wearing his grandmother's wedding ring and holding his baby in her arms. Not a typical fantasy for making love. But he found the thought of being with her—long-term and committed—to be intensely arousing.

Chapter Fourteen

Though Rachel didn't want to get dressed, she shoved her arms into her sleeves and pulled on her turtleneck. Hours had passed since they'd entered the windowless office behind the ice cream parlor, but the time had gone faster than the blink of an eye. She wished these moments could stretch into days, months, years.

In a way, it felt like she'd known Cole forever. There was something so familiar about him. In spite of being opposites, they were well-matched, like a hook and an eye. A bolt and a screw. She chuckled to herself. Best not to think about screws or she'd never get her clothes on.

Their passion was wild. It was crazy. And she knew better. She was an adult—a thirty-something woman who had her life on track. Why had she abandoned all restraint? Was it the intensity of being chased? Did she cling to him because she was terrified that she wouldn't survive this ordeal?

Reluctantly, she zipped her jeans. Maybe the answer was Cole himself. He was different from all the other bad boys she'd known. True, he had an edge. The man earned his living by deception. But he also made her laugh. And he was capable of incredible tenderness.

He smacked her butt and said, "Get your jacket on. If it's not snowing too hard, we need to get on the road."

She was praying for a blizzard. "I don't want to go."

He yanked her into his arms and held her tightly against him. She liked the rough-and-ready way he handled her. He treated her as an equal, not a porcelain figurine that might shatter and break.

"Rachel, beautiful Rachel." His voice dropped to a low, intimate level. "If we had a choice, I'd keep you here forever. I'd burn your clothes so you could never get dressed."

The way she'd burned motorcycle man's leather jacket? "Do you ride motorcycles?"

"Only Harleys."

"Figures."

Pulling away from him, she shrugged into her parka. The superwarm coat felt empty without the added burden of Goldie snuggled against her chest. "Do you think Pearl is okay?"

"We checked with her an hour ago. She was at her friend's condo, feeding the baby."

"That's not what I meant."

He nodded. "It's going to be a long time before she's okay. She lost a daughter and gained a granddaughter. In the space of a day, her whole life got turned upside down."

Like mine. "I'm dressed. What's next?"

"Come with me." He took her hand. "I'm not going to turn on any lights. Somebody might notice."

A shiver trickled down her spine. "Do you think they're watching?"

"Don't know."

They left the office, and he closed the door behind them. For a moment, they stood in the kitchen area and waited for their eyes to become accustomed to the darkness. The empty area with stainless steel fixtures felt cold, even with her parka. She held Cole's hand as he moved toward the front of the shop.

The glow from a streetlight fell softly through the wide, snow-splattered front windows. They circled the serving counter and crossed the white tile floor until they stood at the glass, looking out.

Though it was only nine o'clock, there was no traffic on the main street running through Grand Lake. Snow piled up three feet high at the curb, and a car parked at the side of the road was completely buried. The sidewalk had been cleared enough that two people could walk abreast. On the opposite side of the street, the storefronts were all dark. The town had closed down early.

The light snowfall disappointed her. She'd been hoping for a raging storm that would force them to cancel their plan.

"Looks peaceful," Cole said.

"These blizzards can be real deceptive. I vote to stay here until morning."

He stepped behind her and slipped his arms around her waist. She leaned back against his chest, feeling cozy and protected in his embrace.

"It's pretty," he said. "Maybe your mountains aren't so bad, after all."

She closed her eyes and thought about spending time with him in a ski lodge with paneled walls, a fireplace and a mug of hot buttered rum. "There's nothing as beautiful as a blue sky day with the sun sparkling on champagne powder snow."

"A full moon on a white, sandy beach," he said.

"Mountain streams."

"Palm trees waving in the breeze." He hugged her. "When this is over, I want to take you to California. You can vacation with me."

Her heart took a happy little leap. *He wants to spend more time with me.* Immediately, she pushed the thought aside, not wanting to get her hopes up. "You're just trying to convince me that we should make this drive tonight."

"We'll exit through the back. Then we'll head down the street to the garage behind Pearl's house." He kissed the top of her head. "If everything goes well, this could be over in a matter of hours."

With a sigh, she gave in and followed him through the door at the front of the ice cream parlor into the darkness of the kitchen area.

Cole came to a sudden halt. She couldn't see what he was doing, but she sensed his movement as he raised his gun.

"What's wrong?" she asked.

"The green light on the alarm box is off."

"It must be a malfunction."

"Let's hope so."

They hadn't heard the alarm go off. Though she couldn't see far into the darkness, she surely would have sensed the presence of another person. "There's nobody else in here."

"It's too dark back here," he muttered. "We'll go out the front entrance."

She turned and retraced her steps. He stayed with her, close enough that she felt his arm brush against hers. As she reached the open doorway, the light through the front windows gave her more visibility. She glanced over her shoulder and saw Cole facing backward, toward the kitchen.

When she passed the doorway, she looked toward the front counter to her right. And she froze. The dark silhouette of a huge, broad-shouldered figure stood out against the pale pastel of the wall.

His arms flung wide. "He-e-e-re's Frankie."

He charged toward her, more stumbling than deliberate. His hands slid under her arms and he lifted her off her feet. His forward momentum carried her beyond the counter toward the far wall.

She kicked hard. Her foot tangled with his legs, and she could feel him losing his balance. If he fell, he'd land on top of her with his full weight. He'd crush her.

The instant her boots touched the floor, she threw her weight toward his left. His left shoulder was the one that was injured—the weaker shoulder. The bullet was still in there, probably turning septic.

Frank crashed to the floor, pinning her legs. She struggled to free herself. Frank sat straight up, grabbed her arm and yanked her around so she was sitting in front on him on the floor. Light reflected off the barrel of his gun.

"Don't move," he said. "Neither one of you."

Cole stood only a few feet from them, looking down. His gun aimed at Frank's forehead. "Let her go."

"Yeah? Then you'll drill a hole in my head?"

"If I wanted to kill you," Cole said, "I would have done it back at the cabin."

"You left me there." He coughed. Phlegm rattled in his throat. "Left me to die."

His stench—stale sweat, blood and grit—turned her stomach. A feverish heat emanated from him, and he was shaking. It was clear to her that he was feeling the effects of the gunshot wounds, loss of blood, shock and exposure. He was weakened and losing control. That made him even more dangerous.

Keeping the fear from her voice, she said, "You need a doctor, Frank."

"I need for you to shut the hell up." He pressed the nose

of his gun against her temple. "I can't see a damn thing in here. Turn on the lights, Cole."

"Will the light be a signal for your friends? The murderers you hooked up with at the cabin?"

"I ditched those guys as soon as I got into town."

A spasm shook Frank's body. His gun hand twitched. She was afraid he might kill her by accident. Rachel said, "Do as he says."

"That's right," Frank growled. "I'm in charge."

Cole backed up a few paces, heading toward the light switch by the door. "How did you find us?"

"I met Penny's mom in Black Hawk at the casino. Pearl Richards. She said she was living in Grand Lake. I asked around. Found her house. Went inside. And then...I don't remember. It was warm. Must have gone to sleep."

His grip on consciousness was fading. She wanted to keep him calm and placated. "Finding Pearl was smart, Frank. Why don't you put the gun down and—"

"I'm a hell of a lot smarter than you know," he said. "Ask Cole. I'm good with electronics. Disconnected the alarm to this place. No problem."

"Why did you come here? To the ice cream parlor?"

"Found a business card. I got inside. Easy does it. Then I got dizzy. Shhhhh." He slurred, "Had to s-s-s-sleep."

From the corner of her eye, she saw the gun drooping in his hand. He was on the verge of passing out.

"Let me bring you something to drink," she said gently. "Something nice and cool. You'd like that, wouldn't you?"

His body stiffened as he forced himself awake. "Turn on the damn lights."

When Cole flicked the switch, light flooded the room. The cheerful, pastel décor mocked the hopelessness of her situation. Two men with guns faced each other, and she was in the middle.

Frank shook her arm and ordered her to stand up. "Slow. Move real slow."

She was tempted to bolt. Frank was suffering; his reactions would be slowed. She remembered what Cole had told her earlier. If attacked, hide behind the counter.

"Move," Frank barked.

She did as he said, and he maneuvered into position behind her, using her as a shield. He held her left arm to keep her from running. His gun jabbed her ribs.

When she flinched, Cole reacted. His movements were slight, not enough to spook Frank. But she saw the tension in his jaw and noticed that he had moved a few inches closer.

Like her, he kept his tone level and calm. "You don't want to hurt Rachel. She's the one who's going to lead you to all that money."

"Penny sent the cash here to her mom," Frank said. "It's close. I can smell it."

"You're wrong," she said. "But I'm sure you already know that. You must have searched in the house before you came here."

"Where is it?"

She looked toward Cole, who gave her a nod. Then she said, "Penny sent the money to a friend in Granby. We have to drive to get there."

"If you're lying, I'll kill you." He poked her again. "Cole, put your gun on the floor and step back."

She could guess what would happen if Cole disarmed himself. Frank was desperate, half-crazed. He thought he needed her to lead him to the money, but he had no further use for anyone else. He'd shoot Cole in a minute.

She couldn't stop herself from crying out. "No, Cole. Don't do it."

Frank dragged her by the arm. He edged toward the windows as though he was planning to walk out the front door. Was it unlocked? Had he entered through that door?

"Listen to me, Frank. We'll take you with us," Cole said. "We'll drive together and take you to the money."

"Drop your weapon. Or I'll shoot her in the gut."

"You need her. She's the only one who—"

"Drop it."

Cole placed his gun on the floor.

"That's real good," Frank said. "Kick it over here."

She watched in horror as the automatic weapon slid across the white tile floor into the corner under the painting of the dancing lavender bear in a tutu. This shouldn't be happening. Not here. Lily Belle's Ice Cream Parlor wasn't the place for a showdown.

With a satisfied grunt, Frank pulled the gun away from her side and aimed at Cole. Though his hand wobbled, he couldn't miss from this distance.

She didn't plan her move. All Rachel knew was that she had to do something. She bent forward from the waist. Before Frank could yank her back into an upright position, she flung her head back as hard as she could. Her skull banged against Frank's wounded left shoulder.

He screamed in pain. His grip on her arm released.

She made a frantic dash.

Chapter Fifteen

The gutsy move by Rachel gave Cole the chance he needed.

There wasn't time to reach his gun. Every second counted. He took two quick steps and launched himself in a diving tackle. His shoulder hit the solid mass of Frank's chest, and the big man went down with a thud. Still, he managed to fire two shots. He didn't lose his grip on the weapon.

On the floor, Cole struggled for the gun. From the corner of his eye, he saw Rachel dive across the countertop. She was out of sight. Out of range. Good.

With a yell and a ferocious surge, Frank threw Cole off him and staggered to his feet. He braced his legs, wide apart. His shoulders hunched as he groped the empty air. He squinted. His eyes seemed unable to focus. Like a wounded beast, he swung his long arms, waving the gun back and forth.

Cole squared off with him. A one-two combination to the gut drove Frank backward. Cole flicked a stinging blow to the center of Frank's face, snapping his head back.

His arms flew wide. His fingers loosened. The gun clattered to the floor. This fight was all but over.

Frigid air rushed into the ice cream parlor as the front

door opened. A man with a gun entered. Frank had brought backup, and Cole couldn't handle two of them.

Following Rachel's example, he pivoted and leaped across the soda fountain counter, where he found her crouched on the floor in a tight, little ball. "Are you all right?"

She nodded. "You?"

"Been better."

Three gun shots erupted.

Cole peered over the edge of the counter. Frank sprawled on the floor. His blood splattered the white tile floor.

The gunman flipped back the hood of his parka and said, "It's over. You can come out."

Agent Wayne Prescott.

Slowly, Cole stood. When he'd been looking down the barrel of Frank's gun, he felt less threatened than when Prescott came toward him and extended his hand. There was every reason to believe that this man had betrayed him and put him in lethal danger. Should he shake that hand? Why not just stick his arm down a wood chipper?

"Agent McClure," Prescott said, "you're a hard man to find."

"You've got me now." There was no choice but to play nice. He reached across the soda fountain counter and gripped the traitor's hand. In spite of his years as an undercover operative, he couldn't force himself to return Prescott's smile. "Rachel, this is Agent Wayne Prescott."

His supposedly disarming smile extended to her. "I apologize, Ms. Devon. It's unfortunate that you were caught up in this situation. I assure you that this isn't the way the FBI does business."

Her lips pressed tightly together. With wide, unblinking eyes, she stared at Frank's body. "Is he dead?"

"He's not going to hurt anybody."

Cole knew that her EMT training and instincts wouldn't allow her to ignore a victim. He wasn't surprised when she straightened her shoulders, walked around the counter and knelt beside Frank.

Watching her check for a pulse gave Cole a renewed respect for her. She valued human life—even the miserable existence of someone like Frank Loeb, a man who had tried to kill her. Rachel was a good woman. The best.

She looked up and shook her head. "No need to call for an ambulance."

When Prescott moved closer to her, Cole vaulted over the counter and inserted himself between them. Even though Prescott had holstered his gun, he couldn't be trusted. He looked like one of the good guys with his barbered black hair and clean-shaven jaw. His manner was calm. His expression showed no emotion, typical of a trained agent. Pulling information from him wasn't going to be easy.

Cole helped Rachel to her feet and guided her to one of the padded turquoise stools in front of the counter. When she was seated, he turned toward Prescott, waiting for him to speak first.

Unfortunately, Prescott employed the same negotiating tactic. He stood beside Frank's body as though he was a hunter with a fresh kill waiting to have his photograph taken. The corner of his mouth twitched. Cole could tell that there was something Prescott wanted to know, a burning question that would break his silent facade.

"The baby," Prescott said. "Is the baby all right?"

Cole hadn't expected him to ask about Goldie. If he was right about Prescott working with Baron, the first question should have been about the money.

Rachel answered, "Goldie is doing very well. She's with Penny's mother."

"Where?" Prescott demanded.

Before Rachel could answer, Cole said, "In a safe place."

"I need to see the baby before I can call off the search."

"That doesn't make a hell of a lot of sense," Cole said. "You know we're not armed and dangerous fugitives. You shook my hand. Apologized to Rachel. You put your gun away."

"I'm not the one who made the call for a manhunt," Prescott said. "Somebody higher up said you'd lost it. You know how often that happens with undercover ops."

"Not with me."

"There were three dead bodies. One of them, a woman who had just given birth."

"Who called for the manhunt?"

"The director gave the order. I don't know who talked to him."

A lie? Prescott had jammed his hands into the pockets of his parka so he wouldn't betray any nervousness with his gestures. His forehead pulled into a frown that might indicate concern or confusion. Or else he was hiding something. His dark eyes were steady, but his lips thinned. *Was he lying?*

"You called me in on this investigation," Cole said. "You suspected someone in your office of working with Baron."

"I still do."

Cole continued as though he hadn't spoken. "Then you show up here with Frank."

"Hold it right there. Frank Loeb and I weren't working together. I was following him." He paused. "I didn't know Frank was so skilled at electronics. It didn't take him ten minutes to bypass that burglar alarm."

There was something cruel about discussing Frank's skills while the man lay dead at their feet. Though Rachel was no stranger to violent death, he wanted to get her away from this horror.

Less than an hour ago, they'd been lying in each other's arms. The world had been sweet. He had been happy. No more.

His life didn't have room for a normal relationship. He lived on the razor's edge.

"Call Waxman," Cole said. His handler needed to be apprised of the situation.

Prescott's scowl deepened. "Waxman might be the one who betrayed you. When he assigned you, he warned me that you were a loose cannon. He said that when you go undercover, you cut all ties."

That policy had served Cole well. If Prescott had been able to track him with GPS, he and Rachel would have been caught. "You're saying that Agent Waxman is the traitor."

"I'm not accusing anybody."

But he was pushing suspicion away from himself, which seemed like a blatant ruse. Cole needed to be careful in dealing with this guy. If Prescott had been working with Baron, he had a lot to lose. Not only would his payoff money stop coming, but he'd also lose his job, his reputation and his freedom. The feds dealt harshly with those who conspired against them.

"Think about it, Cole." Prescott's hands came out of his pockets. He held them open, showing that he had nothing to hide. "I'm not the bad guy. If I wanted you dead, I could have killed you when I walked through this door."

A threat? "Don't underestimate me."

It had been a while since he'd killed a man with his bare

hands. The years had taught him patience. He was smarter now than when he first started.

"Here's the deal." Prescott's hands went back into his pockets. "If I call off the manhunt, I have to take you and Rachel into custody."

He looked toward her. She hadn't made a peep. Until now, she hadn't been shy about making her needs and desires known. What was going on behind those liquid blue eyes?

He glanced at Prescott. "Excuse us for a moment."

Taking her arm, he led her toward the door into the rear of the shop. He stood just inside, where he could keep an eye on Prescott while they held a whispered conversation. "Why so quiet?"

"I was watching you," she said. "When you're negotiating, you become a different person."

"How so?"

She lifted her hand as though she wanted to touch him. But she held back. "You know how much I like a bad boy. That element of danger is… Well, it's a turn-on. But you're not the same man who made love to me all day."

"I'm not?"

"You're more like the guy in the ski mask who kidnapped me in my van and stuck a gun in my face."

Though he wanted to give his full attention to Rachel, his gaze focused on Prescott, who stood at the window, staring out at the snow. "That was my undercover identity. You know, like an actor playing a role."

"Actors don't carry real guns."

"True," he conceded.

He wasn't an actor following a safe little script that led to the inevitable happy ending. When he went undercover, he took on another identity. From the way he combed his hair to the way he handled his weapons, he was different.

He couldn't risk showing a single glimpse of himself, and he never knew how it would all end.

"You're scaring me, Cole. You're so closed off, so tough, so cold. Your eyes don't even reflect the light. You're dangerous. And it's a real danger, the kind that got Penny killed."

He could feel her pulling away as though she was walking backward into a mist, fading into a memory. "I don't want to lose you."

"I'm not blaming you. It's your job. It's what you do."

He'd work this out with her later. "We have to make a decision. Do we turn ourselves in?"

"Is it safe?"

"I'd feel better if I knew Baron's identity. I'd have a bargaining chip."

Thus far, his undercover assignment was shaping up to be an unmitigated failure. Four people, including Penny and Frank, were dead. And he was only a few inches closer to finding the mastermind who caused those deaths and engineered a chain of robberies throughout the west.

"You hate to quit," she said.

"Right, again."

"And you promised Pearl that you'd find the man responsible for Penny's murder."

He nodded. "The only way we'll really be safe is when Baron is found, and the traitor in the FBI is identified."

A grin lifted her corners of her mouth. He knew she wasn't trying to be sexy, but that energy emanated from her. "I say the hell with Prescott."

"I've never wanted to kiss somebody so much in my life."

"Kiss me later. Right now, we need to get away from here."

As they returned to the front of Lily Belle's ice cream

parlor, a plan was already taking shape in his mind. He confronted Prescott. "Where were we?"

The pinched eyebrows and the scowl had become a permanent fixture on Prescott's face. "I want an update on your investigation."

"You'll have to wait."

Prescott glared and looked him straight in the eye in an attempt to assert his authority as the higher ranking agent. "You need to start cooperating with me. Tell me what you've learned about Baron."

Cole had two options: keep quiet or dribble out just enough information to get a response. This was a chess game played with hubris and cunning. Spending years undercover gave Cole the clear advantage; he knew how to manipulate people to get information.

He made the first move, starting with the truth. "Baron is the baby's daddy."

Without admitting or denying, Prescott asked, "Will DNA confirm that relationship?" It was a sideways move.

"Penny named him. She grew up in this area."

Prescott's nod was a signal of confidence. "I have background on her. She went to high school in Granby."

"Is that how you tracked her mother?"

"Finding Pearl Richards didn't take any complicated sleuthing." Prescott moved toward bragging. Clearly, he thought he was winning this game. "She had her mail forwarded to the house in Grand Lake."

Cole shot him down. "But you didn't know that the owner of the house also owned the ice cream parlor."

"No, I didn't."

"But you're familiar with the Grand County area," Cole said, remembering what Deputy Loughlin had told them.

"I've been up here a couple of times. I used to be the information liaison for the FBI in Colorado."

A piece of new information. How did it fit? "You did public relations?"

"Checking in with the locals. Giving Q-and-A talks. Creating an FBI presence. In some of these remote areas, weirdo militia groups can take root. It's good if the local people have someone they've met and can talk with."

"So you know people around here." That could be a useful attribute if he was working with Baron. Cole pushed with a more aggressive move. "Is there a more personal reason you've spent time around here?"

"No."

Prescott had hesitated slightly before answering; Cole knew that he'd hit a nerve. The game shifted to his advantage. "Ever owned property in Grand County?"

"This isn't about me." An edge of anger crept into his voice.

"I think maybe it is."

"Damn it, McClure. I offered you a deal to go into custody. I'll take care of you. Trust me."

"I never trust anybody who uses those words."

"My actions speak louder." A red flush colored Prescott's throat. He was getting angry, losing control. "I'm here to help. I didn't kill you when I had the chance."

"You never had that chance." He gestured for Rachel to stay back, out of harm's way.

"Get real, McClure. Frank was charging after you like a wounded grizzly. I had a gun, and you were unarmed."

It was time to take Agent Wayne Prescott down. This was the endgame.

Since they'd both had the same FBI training in H2H, hand-to-hand combat, Cole decided to avoid a real fight.

His plan wasn't to hurt Prescott. Just to show him who was boss.

A pat on the shoulder and a light slap on the ear distracted Prescott enough for Cole to slip his gun from the holster and drop it on the floor. Likely, Prescott was carrying other weapons. Probably had a knife in those pockets where he kept hiding his hands. And an ankle holster.

He blocked a punch with his forearm and waded in closer. Cole ducked. When he popped up, he spun the agent around and pulled off his jacket. He had him in a choke hold.

The whole altercation took less than a minute.

"Here's the deal," Cole said. "I want your vehicle."

"Why?"

Cole released him. "You have to stay here and deal with poor old Frank. And I have someplace to go."

"I'm urging you to turn yourself in. I can't call off the manhunt. Every cop in the state is looking for you, and they are authorized to use force."

"I'm not walking away from this assignment until it's done," Cole said. "Now it's time for you to trust me."

When Prescott leaned down to pick his parka off the floor, he reached for his ankle holster.

Anticipating the move, Cole already had the gun he'd slipped from Prescott's holster pointed in his face. *Checkmate.*

Chapter Sixteen

Fat snowflakes splatted against the windshield of Prescott's four-wheel-drive SUV. A nice vehicle for driving in the snow; Cole understood why Prescott was willing to fight instead of handing over the keys.

As soon as they got into the car, he'd searched the glove box and found nothing but a neat packet containing registration and proof of insurance. Prescott was a careful man. A career agent. He hadn't given up any information, except the part about him being a liaison and knowing people in the area. Somehow that had to be useful.

Though this storm was nowhere near as violent as the blizzard, Cole hated driving through it. He gripped the steering wheel with both hands, willing the tires not to slip on the snow-packed road leading away from Grand Lake. On the plus side, the bad weather was keeping cars off the road. If anybody followed them, the taillights would be easy to spot.

Rachel held his cell phone but hadn't yet dialed. "I don't want to drag Jim Loughlin into this mess. Cole, it's getting worse and worse. You assaulted a federal officer."

"I *am* a federal officer," he said. "A damn site better one than Prescott. And we need your friend to help us."

"Why?"

"I'm pretty sure this nice SUV has GPS. Prescott can track our location."

His plan was to drop off Prescott's car at the house where they were attacked. Like it or not, the feds and the cops would be forced to look at that house and to realize the murders had been committed there. Even a rudimentary crime-scene analysis would show evidence of a major assault. Their investigation would take a different direction—leading *away* from them.

Unfortunately, when the cops checked the property records, they'd see the connection between Xavier Romero and Baron. If Cole wanted to get information from Romero, he needed to contact him before Prescott and his men closed in.

Rachel asked, "What do you want Loughlin to do?"

"Ask him to meet us at the house. He's already been there so he knows the location. I want him to give us a lift."

"Where to?"

"How much he wants to be involved is up to him. Make the call, Rachel. The alternative is another hike through the snow." He dared to take his eyes off the road for an instant to glance at her. "You don't want that, do you?"

As she made the call, he followed the route that he vaguely remembered from the first time the gang went to the house where three of them had died. Navigating in the mountains on these twisting roads that were half-hidden by snow took ninety percent of his concentration. With the other ten percent, he figured out what they should do next.

Initially, he'd thought they would find Penny's friend, Jenna Cambridge, in Granby and pick up the bundles of cash to use as evidence. Now, it was more imperative to hightail it over to Black Hawk to see Xavier Romero. In the past, the old snitch had helped Cole out with information. Romero might be able to cut through the crap and give him Baron's name.

It was becoming obvious that the only way Cole would end this assignment successfully was to apprehend Baron by himself and turn him over to the cops.

"Okay," Rachel said, "Loughlin will meet us at the house."

"Good." He made a left turn. Was this the route? He wished like hell that he was driving on a clean, paved, well-marked California freeway.

"What's going to happen next?"

"I'm going to have a talk with Xavier Romero."

"In Black Hawk? You can't ask Loughlin to drive all the way to Black Hawk."

"I'm hoping he'll loan us his car."

"That's a lot to ask," she said. "He could be charged with aiding and abetting fugitives."

"If we were criminals, he'd be in trouble. But we're not. Remember? We're the good guys."

"I'm an upstanding citizen, but I'm not so sure about you."

That wasn't the way she'd felt when they were lying in each other's arms. She'd snuggled intimately beside him. They were one. Not anymore.

In the real world—the one where she lived in snow-ridden Colorado and he resided in sunny California—he and Rachel were very different people. He lived by deception, and she couldn't tell a lie to save her life. He was no stranger to violence; she was a healer. Different.

And yet, there was a level where they matched perfectly. He didn't quite understand the connection. In a way, she filled in the places where he was lacking. And vice versa.

She gave him a solid grounding. He gave her...excitement. She'd never admit it, but he'd seen the fire in her eyes. Every time they'd been at risk, she had risen to the challenge. He wanted her with him, didn't trust her safety to anyone else, not even Loughlin. But he couldn't ask her to continue on this dangerous path. He needed to do what was right for her.

When he recognized a road sign, he almost cheered. They were headed in the right direction. "This might be a good time for you to take shelter. When I go to Black Hawk, you could stay with the Loughlins."

"Are you trying to get rid of me?"

"I'm trying to keep you safe. Think about it."

Their tire tracks blazed the first trail through the new snow piling up on the road. He would have worried about being followed if that hadn't been his intention; he wanted the cops to come to this house.

"I'm thinking," she said. "If I stay with the Loughlins, I'm putting them in danger. Those guys who attacked the house are still out there."

"The odds are in your favor. Nobody has reason to suspect you'd be with a deputy sheriff."

"But if they guess..." She exhaled a sigh. "This isn't about being safe and smart. Here's the truth. I want to come with you."

He didn't understand, but he liked her decision. "Because?"

"Are you going to make me say it?"

"Oh, yeah."

"I care about you, Cole. I can't imagine being apart from you, sitting around and worrying. Too much of my life has been wasted with sensible decisions. I'm going to follow my heart and stick with you."

He couldn't remember another time when he'd been a heartfelt choice. "I care about you, too."

"Besides," she said, "I can help. You need a partner."

"I've always worked alone."

"Things change."

He made the last turn into the driveway outside the house, put the car in Park but left the engine running. He turned toward her. In the dim illumination from the dashboard, he saw her smile. "Clearly, you've lost your mind."

"Clearly."

He unfastened her seat belt and pulled her toward him. "I'm so damn glad."

WHEN JIM LOUGHLIN pulled up in his four-wheel-drive Jeep, Rachel made a quick introduction. Cole sat in the passenger seat, and she got into the back. During their time on the run, she'd grown accustomed to the way they looked. Their clothes were filthy, bloodstained and torn from catching on branches. Cole's stubble was turning into a full beard. They might as well have the word *fugitive* branded across their foreheads.

Loughlin glanced over his shoulder at her and shook his head. "Hard to believe you're the same woman who helped my sweet Caitlyn into this world."

A lot had changed since then. "How's she doing? Is Sarah okay?"

"They're both great, especially since my mom went home." He put the Jeep in gear and pulled away from the house where the killing had taken place.

Cole said, "I appreciate your help."

"I'd do just about anything for Rachel." He expertly swung onto the road. "She seems to like you. That makes you okay in my book. But I'm hoping you've decided to turn yourselves in and end this."

"I'd like to pack it in," Cole said, "but we're still not safe. There's a traitor in the FBI network. He's working with Baron, and he's not going to let us live. We know too much."

From the backseat, Rachel said, "We need a favor. You don't have to say yes. I'm only asking."

Loughlin drove for a long minute in silence while he considered. She knew this was a hard decision for him. On one hand was his duty as a deputy. On the other was his innate sense of what was right and wrong. Did he believe in her enough to go along with them?

In his deep rumbling voice, Loughlin said, "Name it."

"We need to get to Black Hawk," she said. "We have to talk to a man who—"

"Don't tell me why. I don't want to know." He held up his hand to forestall further conversation. "I can't take you there on account of I need to stay with Sarah and the baby. But you can use my car."

"There's one more thing," Cole said. "We need clothes."

"You're right about that," Loughlin said. "When we get to my house, I'll pull into the garage. You stay here in the car, and I'll bring some stuff down to you. I haven't told Sarah about any of this, and I don't intend to."

"Thanks," Cole said. "I'd be happy to pay you."

"Don't want your money," he grumbled. "Use it to make a donation to Rachel's clinic."

She unhooked her seat belt, leaned forward and gave Loughlin a kiss on the cheek. "You're a good guy."

"Or a crazy one."

She grinned. "There seems to be a lot of that going around."

Settling back into her seat, Rachel realized that she was feeling positive. Crazy? Oh, yeah. Ever since Cole kidnapped her, she'd been caught up in a sort of madness—an emotional tempest that plunged to the depth of terror and then soared. Their passion was unlike anything she'd ever experienced. She wanted to be with him forever, to follow him to the ends of the earth, in spite of the peril. *The very real peril.* She couldn't let herself forget that they were still the subjects of a manhunt, not to mention being sought by Baron's murderous thugs. And they were on their way to chat with a snitch.

None of the other bad boys she'd dated came close to Cole when it came to danger. Why was she grinning?

She only halfway listened to the conversation from the two men in the front of the Jeep. Cole was telling Loughlin about Prescott's role as an FBI liaison.

"He claimed," Cole said, "that he'd met a lot of people in Grand County."

"I recall that some years back there was an FBI agent who talked at a couple of town councils when we had a problem with militia groups setting up camp in the back country."

"Can you think of any other connections he might have?"

"Maybe church meetings. Or Boy Scouts. The idea is to give folks a face—a real live person they can call at the FBI. We do the same thing at the sheriff's department. Right now, we've got a program to get teenagers off their damn cell phones when they're driving."

Rachel had a brain flash. "The high school."

"What's that?" Cole asked.

"Prescott could have given an informational talk at the

high school. I do those programs all the time. The teachers love it when I show up. It gives them a free period."

If Prescott had come to Granby High School when Penny was a student there, he could have met her. Through Penny, he might have linked up with Baron.

In deference to Loughlin's wishes not to know any more about what they were doing than absolutely necessary, she said nothing more, but her mind kept turning.

As soon as they were parked in Loughlin's two-car garage and she was alone with Cole, she said, "What if Prescott met Penny at the high school? Then she introduced him to Baron."

"Interesting theory. But I don't think Penny was a teenaged criminal mastermind."

"From what she told me and what her mother said, she was wild. The kind of kid who gets into trouble."

Instead of pursuing her line of thinking, he grinned. "They say it takes one to know one. Were you a wild child?"

"I had my share of adventures," she admitted. "And really bad luck with the guys I dated."

"Bad boys. Like me."

He left the passenger seat and came around to open her door. In the glare from the overhead light, she realized how truly ratty and beat up his clothes were. In spite of the grime and the scruffy beard, she liked the way he looked. One hundred percent masculine.

She slid off the seat and into his arms. Looking up at him, she said, "You're not a bad boy. Dangerous? Yes. But not bad."

His long, slow kiss sent a heat wave through her veins. Definitely not bad.

Before their kiss progressed into something inappropriate, Loughlin returned to the garage with fresh clothing.

He set the pile of coats, shoes and clothing on his cluttered workbench against the back wall and turned to Rachel. "Could I talk to you in private?"

She went with him through the garage door into a back hallway. "What is it?"

He took both her hands in his and leaned down to peer into her eyes. In a low whisper, he asked, "Is this really what you want? To go with Cole?"

"Yes."

"Rachel, you could get hurt."

"It's worth the risk. *Cole* is worth it."

"You just met this man a couple of days ago," Loughlin said. "You've only known him for a matter of hours."

But she wanted to believe that Cole was the man she'd been looking for all her life. She'd gone through a string of losers—so many that she'd almost given up on men altogether. If she didn't take this chance, she'd regret it. "I'm sure."

He pulled her into a bear hug. "I trust your instincts, girl. Try to be careful."

"I will." His concern touched her. He and Sarah and their baby were like family to her. "Your friendship means a lot."

"Just don't wreck my car. Okay?"

She returned to the garage to find Cole dressed in fresh jeans and a cream-colored turtleneck. Though Loughlin was heavier than Cole, they were the same height. The new outfit was a decent fit.

"A major improvement," she said. "Except for the scruffy beard."

"I thought you liked the rugged mountain-man thing."

"But you're not a mountain man. You're a clean-shaven dude from California."

"Apparently, your friend thinks so, too." He held up an electric razor. "I'm not sure if I should shave. The cops have probably circulated ID photos of me. I don't want to be recognized. On the other hand, a beard could attract closer scrutiny. It's an obvious disguise."

She hadn't considered photos. "Will they have a picture of me?"

"It's possible. But, as you pointed out before, a lot of people in this area know you. If they saw your photo, they'd suspect something was wrong with the manhunt."

"I hope you're right. There's nothing I can do with my short hair except put on a wig or a hat."

He held up a wool knit Sherpa hat with ear flaps. "Ta da."

"I love these." She grabbed it and put it on. "Mmmmm. Warm."

"Warm and damn cute." He gave her a grin. "I was thinking about your theory of Prescott meeting Penny at the high school."

"And?"

"What was the first thing he asked when he found us?"

He had wanted to know about Goldie, wanted to know that she was safe. His concern for the infant was apparent. "The baby."

"Why? Why would that be his first question?"

"He could be the father."

Agent Wayne Prescott might be Baron.

Chapter Seventeen

As they drove to a lower elevation, they left the snowstorm behind. Rachel gazed through the passenger-side window at pinprick stars in the clear night sky. Leaning back in the comfortable seat, she listened to the hum of the Jeep's tires on clear pavement. The only sign of the blizzard that had paralyzed Grand County was a frosting of white on moonlit trees and the rocky walls of the canyon leading to Black Hawk.

The more temperate weather had an obvious effect on Cole, the California guy. His mood was more contemplative. His death grip on the steering wheel had relaxed. The worry lines across his forehead smoothed, and he was almost smiling. With his left hand, he massaged his clean-shaven jaw. Losing the beard made him appear less ferocious and more handsome.

Jim Loughlin had been right when he said she didn't know much about Cole. Even when they were making love, he hadn't talked about his past. Did she want to know? Did she really want to see Cole as more than a casual affair?

Connecting to him on a deeper level was dangerous. He hadn't represented himself as relationship material. Sure, there were the occasional hints that he'd like to see more of her. But nothing he'd said—not one single word—resembled a commitment.

On the other hand, she had taken the ultimate risk when she had unprotected sex with him. Caught up in the whirlwind of their passion, she'd made that decision. Maybe not the smartest thing she'd ever done. Didn't she give lectures to high school classes on exactly this topic? No condom means no sex.

She'd broken her own rule.

For the first time.

Wow.

With other boyfriends, even men she thought she was in love with, she had never once taken that chance. Clearly, there was something special about Cole and she needed to know more about him.

Clearing her throat, she asked, "Did you grow up in California?"

"Mostly."

Not a very revealing answer. She'd have to be more specific. "Where were you born?"

"Vegas."

Now they might be getting somewhere. Cole was in his thirties. When he was born, Las Vegas had been more decadent and edgy than it was now. "Did your parents work in the casinos?"

"Nope."

Another one word response. *Great.* "How long did you live there?"

He turned his head toward her. Moonlight through the windshield shone on the sculpted line of his jaw. "There's no need for you to go on a fishing expedition. If there's something specific you want to know about me, just ask."

"I'm curious," she said. "I want to get an idea of where you came from. How did you grow up to be an undercover FBI agent? What were you like as a kid?"

"I always played with guns." He grinned. "My mom wouldn't let me or my younger brother bring our violent toys into the house. She was a pacifist. A grade school teacher."

"And your father?"

"Dad was a preacher in Vegas—a reformed gambler who started his own church. I can't remember the name of it, but there was a lot of 'repent and be saved' going on."

"You were a preacher's kid." She wouldn't have guessed that background. "If the stereotypes hold true, that means you were either annoyingly perfect or a holy terror."

"I didn't have time to get settled into either personality. I was only five when my parents split up. Marrying my mother and having kids went along with Dad's preacher identity. But it didn't last."

"He went back to gambling," she guessed.

"It turned out that he had a lot of loyal followers, and they donated bundles of cash to build a new rec hall for the church. Dad thought the Lord might help him find a greater contribution in the casinos. Apparently, God was looking the other way."

"He lost the money."

"Not all of it, but a significant portion. The crazy thing was that he admitted what he'd done, and his followers forgave him. Mom wasn't so easy to con. She divorced him and moved us to Los Angeles."

"Did your dad stay in Vegas?"

"For a while. After he paid back the money, he handed over the church to his assistant and devoted himself full-time to gambling. He does okay. He paid child support and stayed in touch with the family. Whenever he showed up, he always had big, extravagant presents."

She was beginning to have a context for understanding Cole. "Were you more like your dad or your mom?"

"I've got a bit of the con man in me," he admitted.

"Which is why you're so good at going undercover."

"But I get my sense of fair play and loyalty from my mom. I never once heard her say a bad thing about my father. She remarried several years ago and moved to Oregon."

"And your brother?"

"He's a fireman. Happily married with two little girls who I love to spoil."

"By showing up with big, extravagant presents?"

He shot her a glance. "I never thought of it that way. Maybe I'm more like my dad than I realize."

"Do you gamble?"

"I'm a hell of a good poker player, but I don't have the sickness. I hate losing too much."

They were on the last curving stretch of road through the canyon that led to Black Hawk. The roads were pristine—well-maintained by casino and hotel owners who wanted to make the trip easy and smooth.

"What we're doing right now is a gamble," she pointed out. "You're taking a chance on being recognized at a casino where you committed a robbery."

"I was wearing a ski mask. Nobody saw my face."

"What if the police put out a photo of you?"

"I've got new identification from the papers I had sewn inside my leather jacket." He shrugged. "If somebody thinks they saw me before, I can talk my way around it."

She wished she had half his confidence. If somebody accused her of being one of the fugitives the FBI was looking for, she'd fall apart. "And what should I do?"

"Say as little as possible. I'm going to introduce you as my associate, even though most FBI agents tend to wear more conservative attire."

The clothing she'd borrowed from Sarah Loughlin was

a size too small. The jeans hugged her bottom, and the pink knit top stretched tightly across her breasts. Even the lavender parka was fitted at the waist. Rachel missed her oversized practical parka. "Too cutesy?"

"Not if you put on the cap with the ear flaps."

"Then I would definitely be too dorky," she said. "Should I have a different name? Can I be Special Agent Angelina?"

"It's better if you have a name you can relate to. Do you have a nickname?"

"My youngest brother calls me Rocky."

"Short for Rachel. I like it. For the last name, let's use the street where you lived as a kid."

"Logan. Call me Special Agent Rocky Logan."

He grinned. "Xavier thinks my name is Calvin Spade. I met him a long time ago, probably eight years, when he was involved in an illegal gambling operation in Culver City. I went in as a card shark, and I did okay in a couple of tournaments. Then I recruited Xavier as a snitch."

She was beginning to feel apprehensive. "I've never been good at lying. Maybe my identity should be something more familiar. Like a nurse."

He reached over and stroked her cheek. "Don't try to play a role. Just be yourself. Go along with whatever I say."

"Roll with the punches."

"Let's hope it doesn't come to that."

The lights of Black Hawk glittered against the dark slopes and the surrounding forest. Extra-large new casinos and parking structures bumped up against the older buildings that had been part of the historic town before limited stakes gambling was legalized here and in neighboring Central City.

Xavier's casino—the Stampede—was at the quiet end

of town away from the new casinos. Cole parked at the far end of the half-full lot. On a weekday night at eleven o'clock, there weren't many cars.

He killed the headlights and turned to her. "If you want, you can stay in the car. I don't expect this to take too long."

Pulling off an undercover identity was daunting, but she wanted to do it. The best way to understand Cole was to see him in action. "I'm ready. Let's go."

As they walked through the crisp night to the casino that appeared to be in a renovated barn, she noticed his sense of humor falling away from him. His posture shifted. His shoulders seemed wider. His height, more impressive.

Trying to match his cool attitude, she narrowed her eyes to a squint. *Agent Rocky Logan is on the job. Bad guys, beware.*

The interior of the casino was similar to an Old West saloon. Rows of slot machines blinked and made clinking noises as though money was pouring out of them. In truth, there were only a few people at the slots. Most of the patrons were huddled around the poker tables.

Cole strode up to the bar. He ordered a couple of beers and asked the bartender—who sported an old-fashioned handlebar mustache—where he could find the old man, Xavier Romero. "Tell him Calvin Spade wants to talk."

The bartender left his post and went through an unmarked door at the rear of the casino. Her apprehension was turning into full-blown anxiety. Her hand trembled as she lifted the beer to her lips. What if Xavier was calling the cops? What if Baron's armed thugs charged out of the back room?

Cole gave her arm a nudge. When she looked up at him, she saw a flash of the familiar Cole—the guy she knew and trusted. He gave her a wink. "It's going to be all right."

She wanted to believe him, but she'd used those very words often when she was dealing with a difficult labor. *It's going to be all right.* An empty reassurance. The pain always got worse before it got better.

When the bartender returned, a short man with white hair and black-rimmed glasses trotted at his heels. He was solidly built but light on his feet. He came to a stop in front of Cole and did a two-fisted handshake. When he smiled, she saw the gleam of a gold tooth.

"It's been a long time." Xavier's voice was a whisper. He swung toward her. "Who's the broad?"

"My associate, Rocky Logan," Cole said. "This is Xavier Romero."

He took her hand and raised it to his lips. "Charmed. When he says 'associate' does he mean you're—"

"We work at the same place," Cole said. "I want to talk to you in private."

Xavier stepped back and gave them both a golden grin. "Take a look around, buddy boy. Finally got my own place. And it's legit."

"The Stampede," Cole said drily. "I never figured you for a cowboy-themed casino."

"Yippee-ki-yay."

Cole said, "I didn't come to talk about the décor."

"We had some good times, you and me. Remember that Texas Hold 'em tournament in Culver City? When I was dating that sweet little redheaded dealer?"

"Didn't come to reminisce, either."

"You were always impatient. Good things come to those who wait. I'm living proof. Seventy years old, and my dream finally comes true."

If she hadn't known that Xavier was involved with

Baron and in the midst of a scheme to defraud his insurance company, she would have liked the old man.

Cole pushed away from the bar. "We'll go to your office. Giddyap."

Though she thought he was being unnecessarily rude, Rachel fell into step behind him. There wasn't enough room between the tables and the slot machines to walk side by side. Xavier hustled to the front of their little parade. He used a key card to open the door and ushered them into a wide hallway with paneled walls and framed sepia photographs of old-time Black Hawk and the gold rush prospectors who populated the town.

The door to his office was open, and Xavier guided them inside. In addition to his cluttered desk, there were a couple of leather sofas and an octagonal poker table covered in green felt. The scent of cigar smoke hung in the air, and she suspected that smoking wasn't the only law that had been broken in this room.

The overhead light, unlike the dimness of the casino, showed a road map of wrinkles on Xavier's face. He sat at the poker table and picked up a deck of cards. "Have a seat."

Cole positioned himself facing the door. "Tell me how you know Baron."

Xavier shuffled the cards with stunning expertise. "Let's play a little five-card stud. No reason we can't be civilized while we talk."

"The last time I played you," Cole said, "I won."

"Give me a chance to get even. If you win again, I'll tell you whatever you want to know."

Cole took the cards from his hand and passed them to her. "Rocky deals."

She knew how to play poker but wasn't an expert. If Cole was expecting her to cheat and give him winning cards, he'd be sorely disappointed. She cut the cards twice and palmed the deck. "Five cards, facedown."

Xavier fixed her with a steady gaze. "Have you been with Calvin long?"

Calvin? Oh, yeah, that was Cole's alias. "Long enough," she said as she dealt.

He tapped his gold tooth with the tip of his index finger. Unlike his weathered face, his hands were smooth. His fingernails, buffed to perfection. "I'm surprised," he said, "to see Calvin with a partner. He usually works alone."

"Things change," Cole said.

"Indeed." Xavier chuckled. "I used to be a petty crook. Now I'm a casino owner."

"Hard to believe that a wheeler-dealer like you is completely legit." He glanced at his cards and turned them facedown on the table. "How did you put together the money to open this place?"

"I know people."

"Baron?"

Xavier checked his cards, pulled out two and slid them toward her. "Hit me."

Cole held up his hand, indicating that he didn't need any more cards. "I'm thinking that you might have used property for collateral to raise cash. A house near Shadow Mountain Lake."

"Or maybe I gambled big in the big game, the stock market. And maybe I was smart enough to get out before the crash." Xavier's wrinkles settled into an expressionless poker face. "If you win this hand, I'll tell you one fact. Then we can play for another and—"

"All or nothing," Cole said. "You don't have much time. All I want is information on Baron. The feds that are going to show up here after me won't be so gentle."

"You? Gentle?" He shook his head. "If I win this hand, you tell me what you know. Then get the hell out."

"I don't lose." Cole's hands on the table were steady. His deep-set eyes radiated confidence. "I'll tell you this for free. Your house near Shadow Mountain Lake was being used as a hideout. People were killed there."

Xavier blinked. "The idiots who robbed my place?"

"The gang was at your house. Not even the dumbest pencil-pushing fed is going to believe that was a coincidence. You were in on the robbery."

"This isn't happening." The old man shook his head slowly. "You're lying. Trying to bluff me."

"Not this time."

Cole turned over his cards. Full house, jacks over tens.

Chapter Eighteen

The only sure way to win at poker was to cheat, and Cole had been learning card tricks from his less-than-holy father before he could read and write. When he'd taken the deck from Xavier, straightened the edges and passed it to Rachel, he'd palmed the cards necessary to play a winning hand.

A simple move. Cole assumed Xavier had been planning to deal himself a winner from the bottom of the deck, so he took those five cards. Voilà! A full house.

Winning was convenient, but he didn't really need that nudge. Xavier was ready to talk; the threat of an FBI investigation into his connection to known criminals had already loosened his lips. He readily admitted that he'd been in touch with Baron when he set up his initial financing. Further, he said that he'd agreed to the casino robbery, knowing that he could claim his missing cash from the insurance company.

"Then everything went wrong," Xavier said. "One of my moron security guards—a guy who's usually asleep in a back room—got trigger happy. Somebody else pulled the alarm."

Cole knew how badly the robbery had been botched. He'd been there. "On the surface, the shoot-out makes it look like you double-crossed Baron."

"It wasn't my fault. I swear it."

Having experienced Baron's wrath when his men peppered the Shadow Mountain Lake house with bullets, Cole was surprised that Xavier wasn't already dead. "There's another piece to the robbery. You're running an insurance scam of your own. You put in a claim for double the amount that was stolen."

"What?"

"You heard me."

Xavier's poker face crumpled. "There's only one way you could know how much was stolen. You were part of the gang."

In order to extract information, Cole needed to balance truth with deception. He had to apply the right amount of pressure and not show his own disadvantages.

Leaning across the table toward Xavier, he said, "You weren't surprised to see me when I walked in the door. You already knew I was one of the robbers. The feds have already sent you my mug shot."

A twitch at the corner of Xavier's mouth confirmed the statement. *He knew.*

Cole continued, "I infiltrated the gang. I was working undercover."

Though confident in his ability to manipulate the old man, Cole had a weak spot, and her name was Special Agent Rocky Logan. Rachel had already told him that she was a lousy liar. He couldn't predict what she'd say.

Apparently, Xavier realized the same thing. He turned toward her and glared through his thick glasses. "What about you, pretty lady? Where do you fit in?"

She narrowed her big blue eyes to a squint—an expression that she probably thought made her look tough. Cole thought she was adorable.

"I advise you to listen to my partner," she said. "He's trying to help you."

"Is he?"

Cole said, "I've got a soft spot when it comes to you, Xavier. A long time ago, you pointed me in the right direction. Do the same thing now. Tell me about Baron."

Xavier leaned back in his chair. "I've never met the man in person. I couldn't ID him if he walked through the door right now. And I don't know where he lives. When I talked to him on the phone, the calls were untraceable."

"It's hard to believe you set up complicated financial dealings without a meeting."

"His secretary handled the paperwork."

Secretary? "You met the secretary?"

"Sure did, but I can't give you a good description. She was wearing a wig and a ton of makeup. Nice breasts, though. She showed plenty of cleavage."

The makeup sounded like Penny. She applied it with a trowel. "How about her age?"

"The older I get," Xavier said, "the younger the ladies look to me. I'd guess that she was in her thirties."

"When did you see her last?"

"A couple of weeks ago. She was with a pregnant woman."

Therefore, the secretary was *not* Penny. Then who? Cole had been part of the gang at that time, but he'd never come to Black Hawk with Penny. A memory clicked in the back of his mind: Pearl had mentioned meeting her daughter here.

Was Penny's mother working for Baron? He didn't want to believe that he'd been so blinded by guilt about Penny's murder that he'd handed over the baby to another crook. When he'd looked into Pearl's eyes, he hadn't seen a hint of deception. She'd been heartbroken about her daughter's death and ecstatic about her new grandbaby. "Did she wear jewelry? Maybe a string of pearls."

Rachel gasped. If she hadn't been thinking of Pearl, she was now.

Xavier pointed to his nicely manicured hands. "Just an engagement ring. A diamond. Not too flashy."

That didn't sound like Penny's mother. She hadn't been wearing an engagement ring when they saw her. Who was this mystery woman? Finding her was the key to finding Baron.

"I played square with you," Xavier said. "What are you going to do to help me?"

"I suggest you call your insurance company and tell them you made a mistake about the amount of money stolen. They haven't made a payout yet. They might let you off the hook."

"Or refuse to pay." Behind his glasses, his eyes darkened. "I need that money to keep going. The whole gang is dead except for you. If you could see your way clear to—"

"Can't do it," Cole said. "We have the loot."

The lie slipped easily off his tongue. But Rachel wasn't so calm. She fidgeted.

And Xavier noticed her nervous move. He zeroed in on her. "Do you? Have the money?"

Before she could stammer out an unconvincing answer, Cole rose from the green felt table. "We're going."

Rachel dropped the cards and stood. Her hands were trembling.

"You don't have the cash," Xavier said. "Baron's procedure is to get the money away from the robbers as soon as possible so they won't get greedy."

"We know where it is," Rachel said. "In a safe place."

The old man sprang to his feet with shocking agility

for a man of his years. "Take me with you. If I can turn in the money and prove that I'm working with the good guys, I could get out of this okay."

"Not a chance," Cole said.

"For old times' sake," he pleaded. "We've got history together. I know your friends. Whatever happened to your buddy from Vegas? That old guy named McClure?"

Moving swiftly and deliberately, Cole came around the table and took Rachel's arm. As soon as he touched her, he knew he'd made a mistake. Xavier would see that his relationship to her was more than a professional association.

He rushed her toward the door. To Xavier, he said, "I'll take care of you."

Instead of making their way through the tables and slot machines in the front of the casino, Cole went to the rear. He pulled Rachel with him through a back door, setting off a screeching alarm.

They ran to Loughlin's Jeep, dove inside and pulled out of the parking lot. As they were driving away, he saw the local police converge on the Stampede casino.

RACHEL HELD HER BREATH as Cole eased out of the casino parking lot with his headlights dark. How could he see? Moonlight wasn't enough.

Sensing a turn, he whipped onto a side road that led past a row of houses. He turned again and headed uphill. The headlights flashed on. He took another turn and another, still climbing. Without snow on the road, his driving skills were expert but scary. She averted her gaze so she couldn't see the speedometer as he fishtailed around a hairpin turn and started a descent. He flew down the narrow canyon road as fast as an alpine skier on the last run of the day.

Across an open field, he drove into forested land. The tall pine trees closed around them, and he slowed.

She exhaled. "How many times in your life have you made dramatic getaways?"

"Often."

Her heart thumped so furiously that she thought her rib cage might explode. Her fingers clenched in a knot. Her skin prickled with an excess of adrenaline. Clearly, she wasn't cut out for undercover work.

Not like Cole. He didn't show the least sign of nervousness. Not now. And not in the casino. The whole time he'd been baiting Xavier, his aura of cool confidence had been unshaken. "How do you do this?"

"Not very well," he muttered.

"You're kidding, right? You were like an old-time riverboat gambler. Sooooo smooth. Always one step ahead, even in that weird poker game. You cheated, right?"

"Yeah."

"If I wasn't familiar with the facts, I wouldn't have known when you were lying and when you were telling the truth. How did you learn to bluff like that?"

"Blame it on genetics. When I first joined the FBI, one of the shrinks told me that I was uniquely suited to undercover work because of my innate behavioral makeup. He gave me a battery of tests, including a lie detector, which I faked out."

"Not surprised," she muttered.

"It seems that I'm a natural born risk-seeker. Most people are risk-averse, more cautious."

"That would be me," she said.

"Not from what you've told me about your boyfriends."

"Okay, maybe I have a risk-seeking lapse when it comes to men. But I'm careful in every other area."

"Being an EMT? Riding in an ambulance?"

"I left that work." Because she couldn't stand the pain of failure. "In every other way, I'm careful."

"And yet, you're riding in a getaway car. You could have backed out at the Loughlins', but you chose to come with me."

She had to admit that he had a point. They weren't total opposites but definitely not peas in a pod. For one thing, she couldn't tell a convincing lie to save her life. "The way you handled Xavier was amazing. You played him."

"But I slipped up," he said. "When we were leaving the room, I took your arm. That's not the kind of gesture I'd use with another FBI agent. And you can bet that Xavier saw that I wanted to protect you. He's no dummy. The old guy knows you're important to me."

"And that's a bad thing?"

"It's a tell," he said. "Like in poker. You never want your opponents to know what you're thinking. I let him see that you're important to me."

In a way, she was touched. In spite of the con, he couldn't keep himself from responding to her. She looked down at her lap and pried her fingers apart. Then she reached toward him. When her hand touched his smoothly shaven cheek, he glanced toward her and grinned.

In that instant of eye contact, she saw his defenses slip away. He really did care about her. She whispered, "What are we going to do for the rest of the night?"

"There are plenty of hotels in Black Hawk and Central City, but they're well-run and organized. The desk clerks might have my photo posted in front of their computers, especially after our escape from the Stampede."

"Right." She frowned. "Why exactly did you rush me out the back door?"

"I had an edgy feeling. When we first saw Xavier, he seemed to be stalling. Maybe he called somebody."

"But when we left, he wanted to come with us."

"I changed his mind," Cole said. "For tonight, I'm thinking of a small motel, a mom-and-pop operation."

Though she was glad that he wasn't planning to drive straight through to Granby and confront Jenna Cambridge, she asked, "Should we go after the money tonight?"

"Too tired. My slip with Xavier showed me that I'm not at the top of my game. I've got to be sharp when we go back to Granby."

Granby. Her home base. She would have loved to take him to her comfy condo, but she was well aware that her home was dangerous. The hunt for them was still active.

"I'm thinking," he said, "that Jenna might be Baron's mysterious secretary."

The same idea had occurred to Rachel. "It makes sense. Penny said that she met Baron at the high school where Jenna teaches."

"If she's the secretary, we could be walking into a trap at her house. Tomorrow is Friday. Jenna will be at the high school, and we'll have a chance to search her place for evidence without interference."

When Penny had talked about her supposed friend, she'd never mentioned a connection with Baron. Though Rachel hated to think ill of the dead, Penny hadn't been very perceptive. She'd cast Jenna in the role of a homely girl who needed advice on makeup and clothing—a non-entity, a sidekick.

The pattern was familiar. A flashy blonde like Penny always seemed to have a dull-as-dishwater friend tagging along. An accurate picture?

Penny's mother also considered Jenna to be a friend, until she found out that Jenna encouraged her daughter's relationship with Baron.

Cole cleared his throat. "There's another woman I suspect."

"Pearl."

Rachel hated that alternative. "If Pearl was working with Baron, why wouldn't she have told him we were hiding at Lily Belle's? We were there all day. His thugs could have attacked us at any time."

He nodded. "My gut tells me Pearl is innocent. But that might be wishful thinking. I've got to believe that Goldie is safe."

"Pearl won't hurt the baby," she said with certainty. "As soon as she took Goldie into her arms, she was in love, and there's nothing stronger than the bond that forms with an infant."

"I'll call her tomorrow morning," he said. "If she's working for Baron, I'll find out."

"How?"

He shrugged. "It'll come to me."

In other words, he would come up with a convincing lie. His talent for deception and manipulation was a bit unnerving; she couldn't be certain of anything he said to her. "Can you teach me how to lie?"

"Why would I do that? I like your honesty."

She wasn't so sure. The truth might be her downfall.

Chapter Nineteen

The adobe-style motel with a blinking Vacancy sign promised low rates for skiers. Since nearby Eldora was one of the closest ski runs to Denver, not many people stayed in the area overnight. There were only four other vehicles parked outside the twelve units.

When Rachel entered room number nine, she felt oddly shy. Though she and Cole had spent the afternoon making passionate love, staying at a motel was different—not because there was a comfortable-looking bed or a shower with hot water. Tonight was planned; they intended to sleep together, and she couldn't claim that she'd been carried away by the drama of the moment. Being here with him represented a deliberate choice. A decision she'd regret?

Every step closer to him deepened the feelings that were building inside her, and it was hard to keep those emotions from turning into something that resembled love. She couldn't make that mistake. Cole wasn't made for a serious relationship. Ultimately, he'd go back to California and leave her in the mountains. They had no future. None at all.

While she opened a greasy bag of fried chicken they'd picked up at a drive-thru, Cole did a poor man's version of surveillance and security. He checked the window in the small but clean bathroom to make sure they had an escape route. Then he shoved the dresser in front of the door.

"What if the bad guys climb in through the bathroom window?" she asked as she pulled out a bag of fries and a deep-fried chunk of white meat.

"They won't," he said. "The lock on the front door is so pitiful that a toddler could kick it open."

"Hence the dresser blockade."

He posted himself at the edge of the front window curtain to watch the parking lot. "Pass me a thigh."

"I had you figured for a breast man."

"I start with the thigh and savor the breast." He tossed her a grin. "But you already know that."

Earlier when they'd made love, she noticed that he paid particular attention to her breasts. The memory tickled her senses. "Have you always been that way? I mean, with other women?"

"You're starting again with the questions." He mimicked her tone and added, "Do you always give men the third degree?"

She washed down a bite of chicken with watery soda. "In the normal course of events, I don't jump into bed with somebody I've only known for a couple of days. There's a period of time when we talk and become familiar with each other."

"Is that so?"

"You might have heard of the concept. It's called dating."

"Touché."

Even though he spent a lot of time undercover, it was hard to believe that a good-looking, eligible guy like Cole hadn't gotten himself hooked once or twice. She asked, "Have you ever had a serious girlfriend? Someone you lived with?"

"You mean like settling down? It's not my thing."

"You must have a home base. A bachelor pad."

"I pay rent on an apartment, but I hardly ever spend time there. It took me over a year to hang pictures on the walls."

She knew exactly what he was talking about. One of her brothers was the same way. He lived in a square little room with a beat-up futon and used pizza boxes for a coffee table. "Sounds lonely."

"Sometimes." He peeked around the edge of the curtain and sighed. "I wish I could have a dog."

Great! His idea of a long-term commitment was canine. "What kind of dog?"

"Border collie," he said without hesitation. "They're smart and fast. And would come in handy if I ever wanted to herd sheep."

Dragging information from Cole was like trying to empty Grand Lake with a teaspoon. "Is that a secret fantasy? Being a shepherd?"

"There are times when I wouldn't mind having a ranch to tend and a couple of acres. Not heavy-duty farming but a place away from the crowds. A quiet place. Peaceful. Where I could raise…stuff." He gnawed at his chicken and avoided looking her in the eye. "Someday, I want to have a family. When I hang out with my nieces, I get this feeling. An attachment."

She remembered his look of wonderment when Goldie was born and his gentleness when he fed the baby her bottle. Maybe this undercover agent wasn't such a confirmed loner, after all. If so, she was glad. Cole was a good man who deserved the comforts of home—a safe haven after his razor-edge assignments.

But was that what he really wanted? A niggling doubt skulked in the shadows of her mind. He might be lying, saying words he knew she wanted to hear. Deception was second nature to him, innate.

Fearful of probing more deeply, she changed the subject. “How long are you going to stand at the window?”

He checked his wristwatch. “Another twenty minutes. There was a sign posted in the office—open until eleven. If they turn out the lights and go to bed, I reckon we’re safe until morning.”

She finished off her chicken and retreated to the bathroom. Not the most modern of accommodations but the white tile and bland fixtures were clean. She shed Sarah Loughlin’s clothes, turned on the hot water and stepped into a bathtub with a blue plastic shower curtain.

The steaming hot water felt good as it splashed into her face and sluiced down her body. Warmth spread through her, and the tension in her muscles began to unwind. She closed her eyes. The bonds of self-control loosened as she relaxed.

Big mistake. As soon as she let her guard down, her mind filled with images she didn’t want to remember. Too many bad things had happened. They played in her head, one after another. Gruesome. Horrible. Sad.

Her eyelids popped open. She tried to focus. Through the plastic shower curtain, the bathroom was a blur.

When she held her hand in the shower spray, she imagined crimson blood oozing through her fingers. Frank’s blood when he lay on the floor of the ice cream parlor. The blood that came when Goldie was born. Penny’s blood when her life was taken.

More blood would spill before this was over. They were getting closer to Baron. The threat was building. Danger squeezed her heart. Not Cole’s blood, she couldn’t bear to lose him. Not like that.

A sob crawled up her throat, and she realized that she

was crying. Her tears mingled with the hot, rushing water. If only she could wash her memory clean and erase her fears.

Her knees buckled, and her hand slid down the white tile wall. With a gasp, she sat down in the bathtub. The shower pelted down on her. The steam clung to her pores.

She heard the bathroom door open. Cole asked, "Are you all right?"

Had she been weeping out loud? "I'm fine."

"The lights in the office are out."

"Great. Close the door."

She didn't want him to see her vulnerability. So far, she'd done a pretty good impression of somebody who could keep it together no matter what. She didn't want him to know that she was afraid. Or needy. That was the worst.

He closed the door but didn't leave the bathroom. "Rachel? Talk to me. You can say anything."

The tenderness in his voice cut through her like a knife. She doubled over into a ball with her head resting on her knees. "Go away."

He eased open the shower curtain. Humiliated by her weakness, she refused to look up at him.

"It's okay," he murmured. "You're going to be okay."

He turned off the shower and draped a towel around her shoulders. The cool air made her shiver. She wanted to move, to pull herself together. But she couldn't pretend that she was fine and dandy. She'd witnessed murders, had been attacked and pursued. Right now, it felt like too damn much to bear.

"You need to get into bed," Cole said as knelt on the floor beside the tub. "Under the covers where it's warm."

"Leave me alone."

His arm circled her back. With a second towel, he dried her face. She batted his hands away.

"Let me help you, Rachel. You're always helping others. It's your turn." His low voice soothed her. "When you're with a woman in labor, you guide her through the pain. That's your job, and you're good at it."

"So?"

"This is my job. The violence. The lies. The fear. And the guilt. It's not easy. If you take my hand, I can help you through it."

She allowed him to guide her into the bedroom, where she slipped between the sheets. Fully dressed except for his boots, he lay beside her and held her.

Though she snuggled against him, she was afraid to close her eyes, fearful of the memories that might return in vivid color. How would she sleep tonight without nightmares?

"I'll tell you a story," he said. "A long time ago, almost ten years, I went on my second undercover assignment. Shouldn't have been complicated, but things went wrong. Some of it was my fault, my inexperience. Anyway, the situation turned dangerous. A man was killed and—"

"Stop." She shoved against his chest. "I really hope this isn't your idea of a cozy bedtime story."

"There's a happy ending," he promised.

"Get to it." She ducked her head under the covers. Her hair was still wet from the shower and she was dripping on him and on the pillow.

"After the assignment, I fell apart. Couldn't sleep. Didn't want to eat. Every loud noise sounded like gunfire. And there were flashbacks. I shed some tears, but mostly I was angry. Unreasonably angry."

"But you're always so cool and controlled."

"I lost it. This little two-tone minivan stole my space

in a parking lot, and I went nuts. Slammed on my brakes, grabbed my tire iron. I charged the van, ready to smash every window. Then I saw the driver—a petite lady with panic in her eyes. There were two toddlers in car seats." He shuddered. "Probably scared those kids out of a year's growth. I got back in my car and drove directly to a shrink."

"You got help."

"Yeah." He pulled her closer. "Having a reaction to what you've been through in the past couple of days is natural. It's all right to cry or yell."

Or curl up in a fetal position in the shower? She appreciated his attempt to let her know she wasn't crazy, even though she still felt like a basket case. "When do we get to the good part of your story?"

"Eventually, you learn to live with it."

"What kind of happy ending is that?" She drew back her head so she could look him in the eye. "I want sunshine and lollipops."

"The truth is better."

"That's my line," she said. "I'm the big stickler for the truth."

His mouth relaxed in a smile. "If you want to cry, go ahead. I understand. And if you want to hit somebody, I can take it."

"Are you sure about that? I hit pretty hard."

"There's no need for you to put up a front, Rachel. You're brave. You're smart. There's nobody I'd rather have for a partner."

As she gazed at him, she realized that she didn't need to explode with tears or screams. She wanted him. To connect with him. To make love.

When she leaned down to kiss him, she dared to close her eyes. She wasn't afraid. Not right now.

His caresses were gentle at first. He tweaked her earlobe and traced the line of her chin. His hand slid down her throat. He cupped her breast, teased the nub, lowered his head and tasted her.

A powerful excitement crackled through her veins, erasing every other emotion. She was torn between the desperate need to have him inside her and a yearning to prolong their love-making for hours. Somewhere in between, they found the perfect rhythm. He scrambled out of his clothes and their naked bodies pressed together.

This was the kind of happy ending she'd been looking for.

WHEN SHE FIRST CAME TO BED, Rachel hadn't thought she'd be able to sleep. The bloody culmination of everything that had happened to them haunted her, and she was afraid of the nightmares that might come.

But after making love, her fears dissipated and exhaustion overwhelmed her. She had slipped into a state of quiet unconsciousness.

She awakened gradually. Last night, she and Cole had once again made love without a condom. Her hand trailed down her body and rested on her flat stomach. Had his seed taken root inside her? Was she pregnant? Other women had told her that they knew the very moment of conception, but she didn't feel any different.

The thought of having a baby—Cole's baby—made her smile. For her, it was the right time. Even if he wasn't the right mate, even if she never saw him after Baron was in custody, she'd be glad finally to be a mother.

She rolled over and reached across the sheets, needing to feel him beside her. But he was gone. "Cole? Cole, where are you?"

"Here."

She saw him standing at the edge of the front window—his sentry position, where he kept an eye on the parking lot outside the motel. The thin light of early morning crept around the curtain and made an interesting highlight on his muscular chest.

"What are you doing all the way over there?"

He sauntered back to the bed and returned to his place beside her. When they touched, her heart fluttered. In spite of her independence, she never wanted to be apart from him.

"I called Waxman," he said.

The last time he talked to his handler in Los Angeles, the man had thrown them under the bus, refusing to help and telling them to turn themselves in. "What did he say?"

"He's coming around." His voice was bitter. "After working with me for years, it finally occurred to Waxman that he could trust me."

"That's good news, right?"

"Not entirely. Without solid evidence, there's nothing Waxman can do about the local feds. Prescott is still running this circus." He ruffled her hair. "Do you like road trips?"

"It depends on where I'm going."

"California," he said. "I want to pick up the loot from Jenna's house, drive to Denver, get a rental car and go home, where Waxman can offer us real protection."

He wanted to take her home with him. She loved the idea. "I'm ready for a trip to the beach."

Chapter Twenty

"In other developments," said the TV anchorman on the early morning local news, "the police in Grand County are still on the lookout for two suspects in the Black Hawk casino robbery."

Cole groaned as his mug shot flashed on the motel room television screen.

The anchorman continued, "If you see this man, contact the Grand County Sheriff's Department. And now, let's take a look at sports. The Nuggets…"

Using the remote, Cole turned off the TV. Apparently, the manhunt was still active but didn't rate headline status. He figured the Grand County cops were plenty busy, processing the crime scene at the Shadow Mountain Lake house and investigating Frank's death—a murder that Prescott would undoubtedly try to pin on him.

Rachel emerged from the bathroom looking fresh and pretty. He liked the way her wispy hair curled on her cheeks when it was damp. Her blue eyes were bright and clear. For the moment, she seemed to have recovered from last night's meltdown, but he knew it would take more time for her to fully cope with the trauma of the past couple of days—trauma that was all his fault, one hundred percent. He'd kidnapped her and dragged her into this mess.

Somehow, he had to make it better.

She'd seemed pleased when he mentioned the road trip. While they were in California, he'd take real good care of her. They'd go for walks on the beach. Or surfing. Or a sailing trip. Or maybe they'd visit his brother. His nieces would love Rachel. He'd show her why living near the ocean was preferable to these damned mountains.

She rubbed her index finger across her teeth. "I brushed with a washcloth and soap. Disgusting."

"As soon as we're on the road, we'll buy toothpaste."

"Or we could stop at my condo when we get to Granby. I actually own a toothbrush. Might even have a spare for you."

He pulled her close and gave her a kiss. Her mouth tasted like detergent, but he didn't complain. "We can't go to your condo. That's the most obvious place for Prescott to arrange for surveillance. And the cops are still looking for us. I just saw my picture on TV."

"What about me? Was I on TV?"

He shook his head. "No mug shot."

"I'm kind of surprised. When the sheriff's men went to the Shadow Mountain Lake house, they must have found my van in the garage. They've got to know my identity."

"They might consider you a hostage." He urged her toward the door. "When we're on the road, you need to turn up your collar and wear the hat with earflaps to hide what you look like. Never can tell where traffic cams might be located."

He was glad to be driving away from the motel. Though the owner hadn't recognized him last night, the guy might remember after seeing the photo on the news. And he might be suspicious if he noticed that Cole had transposed two digits on the license plate when he checked in. He hadn't wanted to leave a record of Loughlin's car being here; no point in getting Rachel's friend in trouble.

In the passenger seat, she stretched and yawned. "It's early."

"Not a morning person?"

"But I am," she said. "I like to start the day with the sun. Look at that sunrise."

To the east, the sky was colored a soft pink that reminded him of the inside of a conch shell. Overhead, the dawn faded to blue with only a few clouds. The morning TV news program had said the weather throughout the state was clear.

He wasn't looking forward to returning to the mounds of snow left behind by the blizzard in Grand County. "How long do you think it'll take us to get to Granby?"

"A couple of hours," she said. "Jenna probably leaves for school around nine. We'll get there a little after that."

Morning was a busy time in most neighborhoods with people going to work and getting started with their day. Since they were going to break into Jenna's house, he preferred to wait until after ten when people had settled into their routines. "We've got about an hour to kill."

"What should we do?"

"Lay low." On the road, they risked being seen on cameras. If he went into a diner or a store, he might be recognized.

"My picture wasn't on TV," she said. "Pull into the next store that's open, I'll run inside and get supplies. Then we find someplace secluded and park until it's time to go."

As good a plan as any.

After a quick stop in Nederland at a convenience store, he left the main road and drove to a secluded overlook that caught the morning sun. One positive about the mountains: it was never hard to find solitude.

Rachel passed him a coffee cup and opened her car door.

"What are you doing?" he asked.

"Come with me."

Grumbling, he unfastened his seat belt and left the warmth of the car. The mountain air held a sharp chill, but he couldn't retreat without looking like a whiner. At least, there wasn't much snow—only pockets of white in the shadows.

He followed her as she climbed onto a flat granite rock and walked to the edge. Stepping up beside her, he took a sip of his hot, black coffee.

She inhaled the cold air and smiled as she looked down from their vantage point. The sun warmed her face. She was beautiful, at peace with herself and the world. No hidden motives roiled inside her. Seldom had he known anyone who lived with such honesty. When Rachel was scared, her fear came from a natural response to a threat. When she laughed, she was truly amused. The woman spoke her mind.

Being with her was the best time he'd had in his life.

Resting his arm on her shoulder, he accepted her vision. Jagged, rocky hillsides filled with trees spread before them. They could see for miles. Sunlight glistened on distant peaks that thrust into the blue sky. Her mountains. Beautiful.

Rachel leaned her back against his chest as she drank her coffee. She said nothing, and he appreciated her silence. No need for words. The experience was enough.

In this moment, he knew. There was no denying the way he felt. He loved this woman.

BEFORE THEY HEADED INTO the high country, Cole needed to make one more phone call. There was, after all, the possibility that they ought to go to Denver instead of Granby. He'd been operating under the theory that Jenna

Cambridge was Baron's secretary, but there was another woman in the picture.

He leaned against the driver's side door and punched numbers into his cell phone. She answered on the fourth ring.

"Hello, Pearl," he said. "How are you doing?"

"Dog tired. I forgot how much work it was to take care of an infant. Goldie was up twice last night for feedings. If she wasn't the most adorable creature in the whole world, I'd be really mad at her."

"We had some trouble at Lily Belle's." His vast understatement didn't begin to describe Frank's attack on them and his murder. "The feds might try to contact you."

"Well then, I'm not going to answer the phone unless it's you. Nobody knows where I'm staying."

"It's smart to keep it that way."

Her instinct to avoid law enforcement reassured him. If Pearl had been Baron's secretary, she'd know about the traitor in the FBI, and she'd use that contact to keep herself out of trouble.

"I miss Penny." Pearl's voice cracked at the edge of a sob. "I keep telling myself that she's an angel in Heaven, looking down and smiling. But she's not here. It's not fair."

"It's not," he agreed.

"You said you'd get the man responsible for my daughter's murder. I'm holding you to that promise."

He wanted nothing more than to see Baron pay for his crimes. "I need to ask you about the last time you saw Penny in Black Hawk. Was there a woman with her?"

"Not that I noticed. That big thug was hanging around, but nobody else."

"What casino were you at?"

"The Stampede. That's the one that got robbed."

Though Cole didn't think Xavier's description matched Pearl, he had to ask about the engagement diamond. "Were you wearing any jewelry?"

"I always wear jewelry. It's free advertising for the stuff I design. But I don't recall what I had on. A couple of rings, some earrings."

"A diamond?"

"Definitely not. I don't use precious gems in my designs."

He switched topics. "Have you ever noticed Jenna wearing an engagement ring?"

"Jenna." She growled the name. "That girl isn't married and is never likely to be. She called me last night, and demanded to know why I hadn't come to her house with the baby. Let me tell you, I gave her a piece of my mind. She should have told me about the older man Penny was dating."

"Did she say anything about him?"

"Not a word. She said she didn't want to betray Penny. I never should have allowed my daughter to spend time with her. It was inappropriate. Why would a high school economics teacher want to hang out with one of her students?"

Why, indeed. "Jenna seems to have a lot of secrets."

"I never thought so before, but you're right. She threatened me on the phone, told me that I wouldn't get custody of Goldie because the baby belongs with her father. That's not true, is it?"

Not if the father was Baron, a criminal mastermind. "I don't think you'll have a problem keeping Goldie."

He passed the phone to Rachel so the two women could talk about the wonderful world of baby care. The fact that Jenna had checked up on Pearl gave him cause for worry. Was she acting for Baron? Was he looking for his child?

No way in hell would Cole allow that bastard to touch one precious hair on Goldie's head. Her survival was a miracle. She had to be kept safe.

When Rachel finished talking, she handed him the phone and gave him a familiar kiss on the cheek. "Pearl and Goldie are okay."

"For now," he said.

She stepped back and regarded him. Her head cocked to one side. Her fists planted on her hips. "Why so ominous?"

"Baron might take it into his head that he wants Goldie. Think about it. The first thing Prescott asked about was the baby. Now Jenna wants to get her hooks into Pearl."

"We can't let that happen." Rachel shuddered. "We have to end this now."

They got back into the Jeep and drove. Though he was glad for the beautiful clear skies, the weather provided nothing in the way of cover. They were exposed. But no one knew they were driving Loughlin's car. With their collars turned up and hats pulled down, he doubted there would be facial recognition on traffic surveillance cams.

When he turned onto U.S. 40, Rachel said, "I have a theory about the engagement ring."

"I'm listening."

"Penny told me that Jenna referred to Baron as Mister Big. A powerful man. An attractive man. Maybe Jenna is more than a secretary. What would you call it? A secretary with benefits? She might be having an affair with Baron, and the ring is wishful thinking."

"If that's true, she would have hated Penny."

"Exactly," Rachel said. "She might be the one who sent those guys to shoot up the house near Shadow Mountain Lake."

Her theory was sound until she got to the shoot-out.

"She wouldn't go against Baron. He's vicious with people who don't follow his orders."

"Then why?" she asked. "Why would he send his men to kill the gang at the hideout?"

"The gang screwed up. Almost got caught."

Baron ran his organization according to strict rules: do as you're told, and you'll profit. Make a mistake, and you'll pay.

"But he almost got his own child killed," she said. "He must have cared something for Penny and she was murdered."

"Collateral damage."

He didn't expect Rachel to understand the workings of a criminal mind. A man like Baron made up his own rules. Penny's murder sent a powerful message to the other people who worked for him. Nobody—not even his pregnant lover—got in his way.

"When you're around someone like that," she said, "how do you keep yourself from showing your emotions?"

"It's my job."

He couldn't explain why he was good at undercover work or why he could beat a lie detector test without breaking a sweat. The FBI shrinks called it a skill. Cole was beginning to think he was cursed.

"Okay." She shrugged. "What do you think about my theory? That Jenna is in love with Baron?"

"I like it." He grinned. "You're one smart detective, Special Agent Rocky Logan."

"It's about time I did something to prove my worth."

"You're the most valuable part of my investigation. Without you, I could never have saved Goldie. It was your connection with Loughlin that got us this transportation. You've helped me. More than you will ever know."

She leaned back against her seat. "This is turning into quite a vacation for me. I can't wait to get to California."

"I have plans for what we'll do when we're there."

In general, Cole considered himself to be good at interrogation and not so much when it came to small talk. But he went at length, telling her about the places he would take her to see and the foods they would sample. "And a sailboat ride on a balmy night. There's nothing like making love at sea."

For once, she didn't counter with a comparison about how the mountains were better. Instead, she beamed a smile. "I know I'll love it."

The long drive into the snow passed quickly. Before he knew it, they were entering the Granby area. He clammed up. Time to put his game face on.

As he drove along the street where Jenna's house was located, Rachel pointed to the address. "That's a nice little place. If I stay in Granby, I might look for something like that."

"If you stay?"

"I'm keeping my options open."

Jenna's cedar frame house with a two-car garage in front was nothing spectacular. An evergreen Christmas wreath hung on the door, and Jenna hadn't yet taken down the string of lights that decorated the eaves.

Cole would have preferred a more secluded location. The house stood on the corner in a residential area with large lots, but the house across the street had a window looking directly at Jenna's front door. The sidewalk and driveway were shoveled, but there was no way they could sneak up on the house through the mounds of snow left behind by the blizzard.

He braked for the stop sign, and then drove on. Though

there were no other cars on the street, he had the sense that they were being watched.

"What's the plan?" Rachel asked.

"I'm not sure yet."

He'd rather not risk being seen, but there didn't seem to be any approach other than parking in the driveway and marching up to the door. If she didn't have an alarm system, he could pick the lock.

Circling the block, he checked his mirrors. Two blocks away, he saw a truck cross an intersection. Nothing else seemed to be moving in this quiet neighborhood. Still, he decided to retreat and consider their next move.

Several blocks away, he backed into a parking space in a lot outside a supermarket. The snow that had been cleared from the lot made an eight-foot-high pile at the far end. Damn this Colorado snow.

He passed his cell phone to Rachel. "Call Jenna and make sure she didn't stay home from work."

"You think we might be walking into a trap."

"Something isn't right."

"I trust your instincts," she said. "I still remember how you sensed the attack on the hideout before a single bullet had been fired."

Before she could make the call, a red SUV pulled up in front of them, trapping them in the parking space.

The back door swung open, and Xavier stepped out. His heavy-duty parka was as red as his vehicle. Stealth had never been his strong point.

He opened the back door to their Jeep and climbed in.

"Hi, kids." His gold tooth flashed when he smiled. "Did you miss me?"

Chapter Twenty-One

Wearing her hat with the earflaps, Rachel doubted she could pull off her super-cool undercover identity as Special Agent Rocky Logan. She turned around in her seat and glared at Xavier. "How did you find us?"

"A good poker player never tells his secrets."

Without turning around, Cole growled, "He must have planted a GPS tracker."

"Where?" she demanded. "How?"

Xavier chuckled. "Under your collar, sweetheart."

Leaning forward, he patted her shoulder, slid his hand up toward her neck and detached a tiny circular object from her parka. Like a magician, he held it up so she could see. "Ta da!"

Though she didn't remember him touching her at the casino, the evidence was there. He had bugged her parka.

She drew the logical conclusion. "That's why we didn't see you tailing us. You knew where we were all the time."

Xavier pocketed the device. "If I'd thought you two were going to stop for the night at a motel, I could have arranged for classier accommodations. But then, you might be seen and recognized. Other people wouldn't be as understanding as I am about harboring a fugitive."

"What do you want?" Cole muttered.

"To get my money back. The insurance company isn't going to be understanding about my losses in the robbery, and I can't afford to be out forty-two thousand bucks."

"Is that right?" She heard the anger in Cole's voice. "Why should I do you any favors?"

"For old times' sake. We go back a long way, buddy boy. You know things about me that nobody else does. And vice versa."

"You don't know squat."

"Come on, now. There's no need to be hostile."

Cole stared through the windshield at the red SUV, and she followed his gaze. The driver was visible through the front window, but she didn't see anybody else. "How many men did you bring with you?"

"Only two. It was never my intention to overpower you. I've seen you in action, and I'm too old to recover from a busted kneecap." Xavier turned to Rachel. "He can be a dangerous fellow. Are you aware of that?"

Since he wasn't treating her like an FBI agent, there was no reason for her to try to outbluff this canny old man. "I know him well," she said. "He's only dangerous with people who need to be taken down."

Behind his glasses, his beady little eyes narrowed. "Be careful about standing too close to the flame, my dear. You might get burned."

Cole turned in his seat to face Xavier. "I don't like the way you followed us. And I'm not making any promises about what happens to the money. But the truth is, I could use some backup."

The old man massaged his chin while he considered. Then he said, "Fine. I scratch your back and you—"

"Here's the deal," Cole said. "Rachel and I are going to break into a house. You and your men wait outside. If we don't come out in ten minutes, it means we need your help."

"I'll do it, and we'll settle up afterward. Aren't you lucky that I turned up when I did?" Xavier opened the car door. "You never appreciated all that I did for you back in the day. It takes guts to be a snitch."

"Guts and greed," Cole said. "Follow us and don't be too obvious."

"By the way." A wide grin split the old man's wrinkled face. His gold tooth gleamed. "How's your wife?"

His wife?

The inside of her head exploded.

Cole was married?

She watched Xavier scamper to his red SUV like an evil leprechaun. She couldn't trust a word he said. He wanted to get back at Cole, to cause him strife.

Desperately wanting to believe that Xavier had been lying, she turned her gaze on Cole. His cognac eyes held a seriousness that she had never seen before.

"Rachel," he said, "I've never lied to you."

That wasn't an answer. She'd asked him dozens of questions about his prior girlfriends and relationships, but she had never actually asked if he had a wife. "Are you married?"

"I can explain."

He hadn't denied it, and she didn't want to be sucked into whatever deceptive ruse he was playing. The man lied for a living. He changed identities every other day. "Yes or no?"

"It's a technicality. No big deal."

She repeated, "Yes or no?"

"Yes."

Anger and hurt knotted in her gut. A flush of heat crawled up her throat and strangled her. Once again, she'd fallen for a bad boy—another man in the long line of dashing, sexy, handsome jerks who ultimately betrayed her. "Don't say another word. I don't want to hear your phony explanations. Let's get this over with and say goodbye."

"Is that what you want?"

"Damn right."

She held up his cell phone and tried to remember how to contact Jenna Cambridge. Pearl had given them the phone number. Was it in the memory? She thrust the phone toward Cole. "Get Jenna on the line."

"I should make this call," he said.

"Because I'm not a natural born liar like you? Because you don't think I can pull it off?"

He grasped her arm near the wrist and pulled her closer, forcing her to confront him. "Settle down, Rachel. If we're going to get through this in one piece, you need to concentrate."

"Don't tell me what I need."

She locked gazes with him. His eyes were intense, volatile. He was nearly as angry as she was, and that was just fine with her. She was done with him and his lies.

With a strength born of fury, she yanked her arm away from him. "Go ahead and call her. I don't care."

While he made the call, she stared through the windshield at Xavier's red SUV. She could see the old man's face in the window of the backseat. He was laughing and she knew the joke was on her.

COLE DROVE INTO Jenna's quiet, residential neighborhood where every sidewalk was shoveled. No one was outside. Nothing seemed to be moving. Beams of sunlight glistened and slowly melted the snow.

He hadn't been able to reach Jenna on the phone, but he'd called the high school and been informed that she was teaching her senior economics seminar and couldn't be disturbed. She wasn't at home; that was all he had to know.

There were still obstacles to breaking into her house. She might have an alarm system or a guard dog or a lock he couldn't pick. *Logistics.* He needed to concentrate on logistics. In normal circumstances, that wouldn't have been a problem. He was good at honing in with sharp focus, doing what had to be done. But Rachel had distracted him.

He glanced over at her. In defiance, she'd torn the cap with earflaps off her head, and her short hair stood up in spikes. A feverish red flush colored her throat and cheeks. Anger sizzled around her like static electricity.

Later, he'd explain about his alleged wife. He should have said something before, but he wasn't accustomed to baring his soul. Damn Xavier for bringing up his wife and making him out to be a liar. Or an unfaithful husband.

Why the hell had Rachel jumped to the worst possible conclusion? It was almost as though she'd been looking for a reason to cut him off at the knees and end this thing that was growing between them. They had a connection, a relationship.

Oh, hell. He might as well face it. He loved her. And she loved him back. But she was as scared of commitment as he was. Why couldn't she understand? He wasn't like all the other creeps she'd dated. He was one of the good guys, damn it.

He shook his head. For now, he had to maintain a single-minded objective. *Get into Jenna's house and find the money.*

In the rearview mirror, he saw the red SUV following them. Tersely, he said, "You should stay outside with Xavier. I'm not sure what I'll find in the house."

"I'm going with you."

"It could be a trap."

"Do you really think so?"

He considered. The evidence connecting Jenna to Baron was largely circumstantial. The only thing they knew for certain was that Penny had sent Jenna the bundles containing the haul from the casino robbery. "Even if she is Baron's secretary, she has no reason to suspect that we're coming after the money."

"So we ought to be fine," Rachel said. "And I'm coming with you to search. Two sets of eyes are better than one."

He pulled into Jenna's driveway and parked. "I go first. If I tell you to run, do it. No questions."

"You're the boss."

"I'm not kidding around," he said.

"You don't need to remind me about the danger." She kept her head averted as though she couldn't stand the sight of him. "I've seen Baron's men in action."

They got out of the car and followed the shoveled path through the snow to the front porch. He saw no indication of an alarm system, but that didn't mean much. Most of these systems were invisible. "We've got five minutes to get in and out. If she has a silent alarm that rings through to a security company, it'll take that long for them to get here."

He pressed the doorbell and listened for any sound coming from inside the house.

Rachel moved along the porch to the front window. "I can't see inside. The drapes are closed."

"Any of the windows open?"

She shook her head. "Triple pane casement windows. They're sealed up tight."

The lock on Jenna's door was a piece of cake, but she also had a dead bolt, which could be a pain in the butt.

He squatted so he was eye level with the door handle and went to work.

"Of course," she said, "you carry a lock pick."

"My version of a Swiss Army knife."

He had the lower lock opened in a couple of minutes. When he pushed on the handle, the door swung open. Jenna hadn't bothered with the dead bolt.

"Five minutes," he reminded her as he took his gun from the holster and stepped inside. "You go left. I'll go right."

He was only halfway down the hallway to the bedrooms when he heard her call out. "Cole."

Something had gone wrong. He whipped around, raising his gun to shoot. A man with a shaved head held Rachel by the throat. His gun pointed to her head.

Cole sensed someone behind his back. A deep voice with a western twang said, "Drop your weapon or she dies."

If he'd been alone, he might have taken his chances with these two. But he couldn't risk Rachel's life. He set his weapon on the floor and raised his hands. "We're not going to cause trouble."

"Too late," the guy behind him said. "We've been chasing you two all over the damn mountains. We halfway froze to death."

If these were the same guys who chased them onto Shadow Mountain Lake, they'd talked to Frank. What had he told them? Cole had to come up with a story that would convince these guys to let them go. Was it better to tell them he was a fed, and the full force of the law would be after them? Should he act like he was still a loyal member of the robbery crew? His mind raced.

He came up with…nothing. No bargaining chip. No leverage. No believable threat. Nothing. Nada. His entire focus was on Rachel. He had to get her out of here. Somehow, he had to save her.

The man behind him shoved him against the wall in the hallway, yanked his arms down and cuffed his hands behind his back. Then, he did a thorough pat-down. When he was satisfied that Cole had been disarmed, he stepped back. "Turn around and walk into the bedroom. I'd advise you not to make any sudden moves."

Cole rooted himself to the floor. No matter what happened to him, he wouldn't leave Rachel alone with these two. "She comes with me."

"Don't you worry none. She's going to be with you. Until death do you part."

The man holding Rachel moved toward them. His arm at her throat was tight.

They went through Jenna's bedroom into the master bathroom. As soon as they were inside, the door closed.

They weren't alone.

Agent Prescott curled up on the floor beside the freestanding bathtub. When he heard them, he opened his eyes and struggled to sit up. Blood from a head wound caked in his hair.

He croaked out one word. "Sorry."

Chapter Twenty-Two

Rachel's nurturing instinct should have sent her running across the bathroom toward Prescott. The man was clearly in need of first aid.

But she wasn't a paramedic anymore. She was the one in imminent danger. She turned toward Cole and placed the flat of her hand on his chest. *Until death did them part?* They weren't going to get out of this alive. The guys who nabbed them were the same merciless bastards who mowed down the gang at the Shadow Mountain Lake house. "Why didn't they kill us when we walked in the door?"

When he looked down at her, his gaze was so warm and full of caring that her heart ached. "Murder leaves a mess," he said. "That's why we're in a bathroom. If they kill us here, they can swab down the tiles and get rid of the evidence."

"That can't be right."

"Why not?"

How could she be discussing the circumstances of her own death? With ridiculous calm, she said, "There'd still be evidence. The CSI shows on TV always find traces."

"I seriously doubt the Grand County Sheriff's Department has a mass spectrometer or instant DNA analysis."

"But you and Prescott are FBI. You guys have all the forensic goodies."

He gave her a sad smile. Then he looked at Prescott. "You're in the Denver office. Do you think they're good enough to figure out who killed us?"

Using the edge of the tub, Agent Prescott forced himself to stand. His breathing was shallow. Even from a distance, she could tell that his pupils were dilated. "You're in shock," she said. "You're probably concussed and should be in a hospital."

He reached up and touched the wound on his head. His fingers came away bloody. "Tell me about Goldie. Is my baby girl safe?"

His baby? "You're Goldie's father?"

"Son of a bitch," Cole muttered. "I underestimated you, Prescott. I thought you were nothing more than a scumbag traitor, but I was wrong. You're the big man himself. You're Baron."

Prescott wiped his bloody hand across his mouth, leaving a streak of crimson. "Not by choice."

Cole looked down at her. "Get the lock picks from my jacket pocket and put them in my hands. I need to get out of these cuffs."

Moments ago, she'd been complaining about the fact that he carried tools for a break-in. Now, she was glad. "Tell me how to do it. I can help."

"It's faster if I handle it myself. This isn't the first time I've been in this position."

When she reached inside his jacket, her physical connection with him was immediate and intimate. She couldn't deny their chemistry. Not that it mattered. Even if she forgave his deception and admitted how much she cared about him, they were going to be dead. "What's going to happen to us?"

Prescott answered, "They'll load us in a car, drive to the mountains, kill us and bury our bodies. We won't be found until the spring thaw. By then, Jenna will be long gone."

She placed the picks in Cole's hands and turned toward Prescott. He seemed to be regaining strength. From experience, she knew that head wounds were unpredictable. He might have a surge of coherence, might even appear to be making a recovery. Or he might collapse into a coma.

"You're Baron," she said. "Why can't you stop them?"

"I don't call the shots. Jenna is in charge. She's always been the boss. Ever since I first met her."

"Was that when you came to the high school in Granby to lecture about the FBI?"

"Before that." He winced. "Jenna lived in Denver. We were engaged."

That explained the ring she still wore. "After you broke up, she moved to the mountains."

Rachel understood the need for a change of scenery. She'd done much the same thing when she joined Rocky Mountain Women's Clinic as a midwife. Like Jenna, she'd been searching for a place to start over.

Prescott said, "She invited me to Granby to talk to her class. That's when I met Penny. Poor, sweet Penny. I was attracted to her right away, but she was a high school kid. Too young. I wooed her. Gave her presents."

"A diamond tennis bracelet," Rachel said.

"I picked it up at a pawn shop, but she didn't know that. She thought I was her true love, her soulmate. All that lovey-dovey crap. And here's the funny part." He inhaled and straightened his shoulders. "I felt the same damn way. I waited until she was ready. I swear to God, I didn't make love to her until she was eighteen."

"Real decent of you," Cole muttered. "How did you get hooked up with Jenna again?"

"She pretended to be my friend. And Penny's. But she was scheming. Spinning her web. Like a spider. A black widow spider. A poisonous creature who..."

His words faded, and she could see him slipping toward unconsciousness. If he passed out, there was a good chance he wouldn't wake up. She went toward him, grabbed his arm and shook him. "Stay with me, Prescott. Tell me about Jenna."

"She's smart. Cunning. Has a master's degree in economics. She put together the whole robbery and money-laundering scheme."

"Interesting," Cole said. "Her logistics were complicated but kind of genius. How did she pull it off?"

"Untraceable email. Throwaway phones. She pretended to be a secretary and invented a boss nobody saw. Baron."

"How did you get involved?"

"She needed to hide behind a frontman. So she set me up with fake deposits to an account in my name. When we were engaged, she handled my bills, got my social security number, all my passwords. By the time she told me about it, there was enough evidence against me to destroy my career and my life."

"You should have turned her in," Cole said.

"I wanted to. But she had Penny on the hook. If I didn't do what Jenna said, Penny would pay the price."

The long confession seemed to invigorate him. Instead of growing weaker, his voice sounded determined. "When I found out that Penny was pregnant, I started making plans to run away with her. We could have had a decent life. Could have raised our baby. Could have—"

A burst of gunfire echoed from the other room.

Cole broke free. The cuffs dangled from his left wrist, but his hands were separated. "Let's get the hell out of here."

She didn't see an escape. The only window in the bathroom was glass bricks—the kind you can't break without a jackhammer.

"What's happening?" Prescott demanded. "Who's shooting?"

"We brought backup," Cole said. "But I don't trust them to be effective. We've got to get out of the bathroom. If those guys catch us in here, it'll be like shooting fish in a barrel."

He eased open the bathroom door. Over his shoulder, he whispered, "I don't see a guard."

If she'd had time to think, she would have been terrified, but everything was happening too fast. Cole grabbed her hand and pulled her behind him into Jenna's bedroom.

She scanned the room, looking for a place to hide. Under the king-size four-poster bed? In the closet? There was a lot of large, heavy furniture in dark wood. Floor-to-ceiling curtains hung beside two windows. Both had decorative security bars on the outside.

Shouts and more gunfire echoed from the front of the house. Cole peeked into the hallway and came back to her. "If we go that way, they'll see us."

He pulled her into the walk-in closet and closed the door. The closet was as big as a bedroom. A scent of cedar and cinnamon hung in the air.

Cole turned on the overhead light. The closet system combined hanging racks, drawers and shelving. Against the back wall were shoes, hats and a shelf with three wigs—black, blond and auburn. Jenna's disguises. Nothing was out of place. Everything was meticulously organized.

It seemed almost sacrilegious when Cole scooped the clothes off a low rack and took the pole where they had been hanging. He did the same with another pole and handed it to her.

"Weapons," he said.

Wooden dowels wouldn't be much use against bullets, but it was better than nothing. He pulled her to a position beside the door and whispered, "I need to explain about my wife."

"Not now. It's not important."

"This might be the last thing I ever say to you, and I want you to know that I'm not a liar or a cheat. The marriage was years ago. I was investigating the illegal gambling scene in California, and I had a female partner. There were problems with our undercover identities. Somehow, we ended up going through a wedding ceremony and signing papers that I suppose are still legal. But there was never anything romantic between us."

"Why should I believe you?"

"I never had to mention this phony marriage to you. But I'm trying to be honest. To tell you everything."

"So, what happened with this partner of yours?"

"She transferred back east. Neither of us bothered with a divorce. I didn't see a need. There wasn't anyone else in my life. Not until now. Not until you."

She heard more gunfire from the other room. There was no way out of this mess.

"That's a mighty strange story," she said.

"It's the truth."

A fake marriage to a partner? An unconsummated marriage? Not bothering with a divorce? If she hadn't gone through the past days with Cole and seen how many twists and turns his life involved, she would have dismissed his story. But she knew his life was complicated. Crazy. Wild. "I believe you."

"I love you, Rachel."

Her arms closed around him. She wanted to be strong and brave, didn't want to cry. But tears spilled down her cheeks. "I love you, too."

This might be the last time they embraced. She'd found love only to lose it.

"When we get out of this," he said, "I'll get a divorce and marry you."

"That's a hell of a way to propose." She scrubbed the moisture from her face. "What if I say no?"

"That's not an option."

The shooting stopped abruptly. She heard voices from the other room.

Cole turned off the overhead light in the closet and stepped in front of her. "Stay back," he said. "No matter what happens, stay in here."

The voices came closer. One was a woman. Jenna?

The closet door whipped open. Cole reacted. He swung hard with the dowel, striking the gun of the man who opened the door. He dropped his weapon. Cole dove, trying to reach the gun.

He was out of her line of sight. She heard shots being fired.

Then silence.

Panic roared through her. Without thinking, she charged through the open door with her dowel raised to strike.

The scene before her was a tableaux. Cole stood

between Prescott and a mousy woman in a button-down shirt, striped vest and gray slacks. They both had their weapons aimed at him.

On the floor in front of Cole, another man lay bleeding.

"Drop your weapons," Prescott ordered. "Both of you."

Cole glanced at her and gave a nod as he dropped his dowel on the floor. "It's okay, Rachel."

"No." She refused to give up. "It's not okay."

"We can negotiate," Prescott said. "Nobody else has to die."

Rachel pointed her dowel at the woman. "I want to hear from her. Jenna Cambridge."

Jenna looked down her long nose. "Don't be stupid. I might decide to let you go after you've served your purpose as a hostage. I don't particularly want to kill you."

"Not like Penny?"

Jenna's dull brown eyes flicked nervously from left to right, but her gun hand remained steady. "That shouldn't have happened."

"Convenient for you that it did," Rachel said. "With Penny out of the way, your former fiancé can come back to you."

"I told you once not to be a fool," Jenna said in a teacherlike voice. "I won't tell you again."

"You won't get away with this."

"I'm a good planner." She glanced toward Prescott. "We're going away together. We'll have a new life with enough money that we won't ever have to work again. I've worked hard and I deserve that much, don't I, darling?"

Prescott crossed the room and stood before her. "You deserve something."

"There's only one thing I've ever wanted," she said with a simpering grin. "Your love."

"Sorry, Jenna. I already gave my heart."

He shoved his gun against her rib cage and pulled the trigger. She gasped. And fell.

She was dead before she hit the floor.

He tried to turn the gun on himself, but Cole was too fast. He wrenched the weapon from Prescott's hand. With surprising gentleness, he guided the wounded agent to the bed.

Prescott sat with his head drooped forward. "She would have killed you. Couldn't let that happen."

Cole patted his shoulder. "You came through when I needed you. I won't forget that."

"My life is over."

"Not yet," Cole said. "You have a baby."

"Goldie." He lifted his head. "Penny's baby."

"You need to see her and hold her. But first, you've got to get us out of this mess. The cops still think Rachel and I are fugitives."

"I'll take care of it." Prescott rose. He wavered for a moment before he straightened and walked toward the front of the house. "The police should be here any minute. As soon as I got out of the bathroom, I put in a call."

Eager to leave the carnage in the bedroom, Rachel followed him. She didn't get far. In the hallway, Cole caught hold of her hand and spun her around to face him. His hands rested at her waist.

He smiled down at her. "When you came charging out of the closet, you scared me."

"I think you have that backwards. I was scared." She remembered how he'd told her that eventually the trauma would fade. "I guess our road trip to California is off."

"Hell, no. I'm not letting you out of my sight." He dropped a kiss on her forehead. "The world is a dangerous place. I need to protect my bride-to-be."

There were a million details to work out, but nothing seemed important. They were together. They were safe, and she wanted to keep it that way forever.

Epilogue

Nine months later, Rachel draped her wedding gown over her swollen belly. Turning sideways, she admired her profile in the full-length mirror in her bedroom. Pregnancy suited her well.

After a quick tap on the door, Cole slipped inside. She was too big for a normal embrace, but he managed to wrap his arms around her. "How's my bride?"

"Good." She'd felt a bit of cramping earlier. It might be a good idea to hurry. "And my groom?"

"Never better."

Given the fact that he was an uncompromising man, he'd been incredibly cooperative about making changes in his life. After the betrayal by his handler in California, Cole didn't want to return to the Los Angeles office of the FBI. He still loved the sun and the beach, but he decided that being a mountain man wasn't so bad.

Prescott's arrest had left an opening in the Denver office, and Cole stepped in to fill it. He still did undercover assignments, but much of his workload fell under the category of investigation. He was considered a rising star because he had not only put the Baron theft ring out of business but had also recovered the stolen cash.

She had also made concessions. Granby was too far from his work, so she moved closer to Denver and opened a new branch for the Rocky Mountain Women's Clinic. When they bought their house in Idaho Springs, Cole had one stipulation. Twice a year, they would vacation on a beach.

Everything seemed to be working out neatly. Except for the wedding. She'd wanted a small ceremony, but things had gotten out of hand. All of her huge family was there as well as Cole's brother's family, his mother and his silver-haired gambler father, who was one of the most charming men she'd ever met. Cole's dad was making quite an impression on Pearl, who had full custody of Goldie the Miracle Baby.

As they made plans, the guest list multiplied. They couldn't leave out the people she'd worked with and the parents of the babies she'd delivered. Nor could they ignore Cole's coworkers. And then there were friends, including Xavier, who had gotten off with little more than a slap on the wrist for his involvement with Baron. She didn't resent the casino owner. How could she? He and his men had provided the gunfire and distraction that had saved their lives.

She kissed Cole on the cheek. In his black suit and white shirt, he was so handsome. Was she really getting married to this gorgeous man?

"How's the crowd?" she asked.

"Restless," he said. "Most of them have already left for the church. I should be going, too. But I wanted to see you one more time before we say our vows."

"Having second thoughts?"

"Hell, no. I just wanted to tell you how much you mean to me. I never imagined I could be so happy. And that's the truth."

"I love you, Cole."

When she reached up to stroke his cheek, the ache in her

abdomen became more intense, more prolonged. Rachel knew the signs; she was going into labor.

"Something wrong?" he asked.

"Everything is right." She looked up at her husband-to-be and smiled. "It's time."

For the first time since the moment they met, she saw sheer panic in his eyes. He gaped. He gasped. He ran to the door. Then back to her. "Are you sure?"

She nodded. "This is what I do."

He placed one hand on her belly, leaned down and kissed her. "It's going to be all right."

And it was.

* * * * *

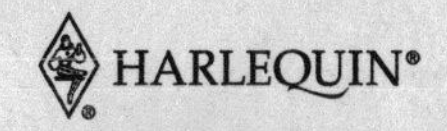

INTRIGUE®

COMING NEXT MONTH

Available February 8, 2011

#1257 SEIZED BY THE SHEIK
Cowboys Royale
Ann Voss Peterson

#1258 SCENE OF THE CRIME: BACHELOR MOON
Carla Cassidy

#1259 DARKWOOD MANOR
Shivers
Jenna Ryan

#1260 GUNNING FOR TROUBLE
Mystery Men
HelenKay Dimon

#1261 BRAZEN
The McKenna Legacy
Patricia Rosemoor

#1262 .38 CALIBER COVER-UP
Angi Morgan

HICNM0111

Spotlight on

Classic

Quintessential, modern love stories that are romance at its finest.

See the next page to enjoy a sneak peek from the Harlequin® Romance series.

CATCLASSHR10

Harlequin Romance author Donna Alward is loved for her gorgeous rancher heroes.

Meet Wyatt as he's confronted by both a precious little pink bundle left on his doorstep and his neighbor Elli who's going to show him the ropes....

Introducing
PROUD RANCHER, PRECIOUS BUNDLE

THE SQUAWKING QUIETED as Elli picked the baby up, and Wyatt turned around, trying hard to ignore the feelings of inadequacy as Darcy immediately stopped fussing.

"Maybe she's uncomfortable. What do you think, sweetheart?" Elli turned her conversation to the baby.

"What do you think is wrong?" Wyatt asked, putting the coffee pot back on the burner.

A strange look passed over Elli's face, one that looked like guilt and panic. But it was gone quickly. "I couldn't say," she replied.

"But you were so good with her this afternoon." Wyatt put his hands on his hips.

"Lucky, that's all. I just...remembered a few things." The same strange look flitted over her features once more.

Wyatt took the coffee to the table. "You fooled me. You looked like you knew exactly what you were doing." So much so that Wyatt had felt completely inept. A feeling he despised. He was used to being the one in control.

Elli and Darcy walked the length of the kitchen and back. After a few moments, she admitted, "I haven't really cared for a baby before. The things I thought of were simply things I'd heard about. Not from experience, Mr. Black."

Her chin jutted up, closing the subject but making him

HREXP0211

want to ask the questions now pulsing through his mind. But then he remembered the old saying—*Don't look a gift horse in the mouth.* He'd benefit from whatever insight she had and be glad of it.

"I don't really know what babies need," he said. "I fed her, patted her back like you did, walked her to sleep, but every time I put her down…"

Wyatt almost groaned. Of course. He'd forgotten one important thing. He'd been so focused on getting the formula the right temperature that he'd forgotten to check her diaper. Not that he had any clue what to do there either.

Pulling calves and shoveling out stalls was far less intimidating than one tiny newborn.

"She's probably due for a diaper change, isn't she." He tried to sound nonchalant. This was a perfect opportunity. Elli must know how to change a diaper. He could simply watch her so he'd know better for the next time.

Instead, Elli came around the corner of the counter and placed Darcy back in his arms. "Here you go, Uncle Wyatt," she said lightly. "You get diaper duty. I'll fix the coffee. Cream and sugar?"

Oh boy, Wyatt thought, looking down into Darcy's pursed face, his smug plan blown to smithereens. He was in for it now.

Will sparks fly between Elli and Wyatt?

Find out in
PROUD RANCHER, PRECIOUS BUNDLE
Available February 2011 from Harlequin Romance

HREXP0211

Try these Healthy and Delicious Spring Rolls!

INGREDIENTS	DIRECTIONS
2 packages rice-paper spring roll wrappers (20 wrappers)	1. Soak one rice-paper wrapper in a large bowl of hot water until softened.
1 cup grated carrot	2. Place a pinch each of carrots, sprouts, cucumber, bell pepper and green onion on the wrapper toward the bottom third of the rice paper.
¼ cup bean sprouts	3. Fold ends in and roll tightly to enclose filling.
1 cucumber, julienned	4. Repeat with remaining wrappers. Chill before serving.
1 red bell pepper, without stem and seeds, julienned	
4 green onions finely chopped—use only the green part	